EDWARD UPWARD was born in 1903 at Romford, Essex, and educated at Repton and at Corpus Christi College, Cambridge, where he read English and History, and was awarded the Chancellor's Medal for English Verse. While at Cambridge he created with Christopher Isherwood a series of stories about the fictitious village of Mortmere. After graduating he became a schoolmaster; from 1931 until his retirement in 1961 he taught at Alleyn's School, Dulwich, where he was a housemaster and head of the English department.

Edward Upward's first novel, *Journey to the Border*, was originally published by Leonard and Virginia Woolf at the Hogarth Press in 1938. In the 1930s he also contributed stories to *New Country, New Writing* and the *Left Review* and was on the editorial board of *The Ploughshare*, journal of the Teachers' Anti-War Movement. For sixteen years he was a member of the Communist Party of Great Britain, but he left it in 1948 because he believed it was ceasing to be a Marxist party.

Between 1942 and 1961 Upward wrote nothing, mainly for political reasons, but in 1962 Heinemann published *In the Thirties*, the first part of his trilogy of novels *The Spiral Ascent*. The second part, *The Rotten Elements*, and the third, *No Home but the Struggle*, were published in 1969 and 1977. Edward Upward's other books include *The Railway Accident and Other Stories* (1969), *The Night Walk and Other Stories* (1987), and in this Enitharmon series, *The Mortmere Stories, An Unmentionable Man*, a revised version of *Journey to the Border* (all published in 1994), and the memoir *Christopher Isherwood: Notes in Remembrance of a Friendship* (1996).

EDWARD UPWARD

The Scenic Railway

London
ENITHARMON PRESS
1997

First published in 1997 by the Enitharmon Press
36 St George's Avenue, London N7 0HD

Distributed in Europe by Password (Books) Ltd
23 New Mount Street, Manchester M4 4DE

Distributed in the USA and Canada by Dufour Editions Inc.
PO Box 449, Chester Springs, Pennsylvania 19425, USA

ISBN 1 900564 65 3   (paper)
ISBN 1 900564 70 X   (cloth edition, limited to 50 copies,
numbered and signed by Edward Upward,
and bound by The Fine Bindery)

British Library Cataloguing-in-Publication Data.
A catalogue record for this book is available from the British Library.

Set in Bembo by Sutchinda Rangsi-Thompson.
Printed in Great Britain by
The Cromwell Press, Broughton Gifford, Wiltshire

BOOKS BY EDWARD UPWARD

Journey to the Border (Hogarth Press, 1938)

•••

THE SPIRAL ASCENT: A TRILOGY

In the Thirties (Heinemann, 1962; Penguin Books, 1969)
The Rotten Elements (Heinemann, 1969; Penguin Books, 1972)
No Home but the Struggle (Heinemann, 1977)

The Spiral Ascent was also published in one volume
by Heinemann in 1977, and reissued in three
paperback volumes by Quartet in 1978–79.

•••

The Railway Accident and Other Stories (Heinemann, 1969;
Penguin Modern Classics, 1972 and 1988)

The Night Walk and Other Stories (Heinemann, 1987)

•••

Journey to the Border – a revised version (Enitharmon, 1994)
introduced by Stephen Spender

An Unmentionable Man (Enitharmon, 1994)
introduced by Frank Kermode

with Christopher Isherwood
The Mortmere Stories (Enitharmon, 1994)
introduced by Katherine Bucknell

Christopher Isherwood: Notes in Remembrance of a Friendship
(Enitharmon, 1996)

ACKNOWLEDGEMENTS

'The Scenic Railway' first appeared in *London Magazine* (June 1988) and was reprinted in *Best Short Stories* of 1989 (Heinemann, 1989) and as 'Paesaggi di cartapesta' in *Linea d'Ombra*, no. 73 (August 1992). 'Investigation after Midnight' and 'People Hate Me' appeared in *London Magazine* (April/May 1990; October/ November 1991).

Note on the text

The stories are presented in the order in which they were written:

'The Scenic Railway' June 1987
'Investigation After Midnight' April 1989
'People Hate Me' April 1991
'The World Revolution' January 1996
'Emily and Oswin' October 1996

Contents

THE SCENIC RAILWAY

T HE EARLY AFTERNOON was warmly bright, the grey-white autumnal clematis was profuse on the roadside hedges, the views of sea and country became more extensive as the car went up the hill, and the tones of the voices of the five disabled passengers who were being driven by Leslie Brellis to the Happiland Amusement Park were cheerfully expectant; but Leslie began to suspect he might not have fully recovered yet from the attack of giddiness he'd had soon after getting out of bed this morning. When the trees of the Park, with the red-and-white-striped dome of the Pleasure Palace conspicuous among them, came into sight not far ahead in a valley descending steeply to the coastline below the hill, he noticed that the dome appeared to sway slightly as if shaken by a minor earth tremor, though the high cedars around it were quite unmoved. The appearance might be due to a trick of the afternoon sunlight on the spirally twisted stripes of the dome. But if the swaying he seemed to see had no objective reality at all, not even the reality of an externally caused deceptive appearance, and was due solely to the distortion of his seeing by a dizzy shakiness in himself, he ought not to be driving these disabled people in this car. Perhaps he ought to stop at once.

He thought of asking Willie Tyler, who sat beside him staring raptly ahead through the windscreen of the car, some not too particularised question which would lead Willie to reveal whether he too had noticed an apparent swaying of the dome. But Willie was an inveterate romancer and quite capable, if he guessed what Leslie was trying to find out, of saying he was sure the dome was moving up and down as well as from side to side. Also an answer of any kind from Willie would take time to get, because he had a speech defect, a stammer which every now and then when he seemed to be speaking almost easily would bring him to a dead stop, with his mouth open, agonisingly trying to utter a next word and absolutely unable to say anything more until someone else spoke the word for him and he was gratefully able to go on again. And Leslie in any case did not really need to ask Willie about the dome. He was becoming all too certain that its swaying was an illusion produced by his own physical state. But he knew that if he stopped his large estate car anywhere here on this narrow curving road along the hillside it would be a hazard to other traffic.

He drove on, much more slowly than before. He realised how right his wife Lana had been at breakfast to warn him that his vertigo this morning, like his similar attack last month, was mainly caused by his putting extra pressure on himself recently and that he must give up this weekly driving he had volunteered to do for a local 'caring' organisation, or else he would become incapable of going on any longer with the political activities which had mattered more than anything else to him and to her ever since their retirement to the South Coast fifteen years before. But by the end of breakfast, though he had promised her he would not drive for the organisation again after today, he had told her he mustn't fail to transport his disabled group this afternoon, because their outing to the Happiland Park was the one they looked forward to above every other in the year. And now on this narrow road along the hillside he might at any moment, owing to an optical misjudgement, steer the car over the edge of the road and plunge it with himself and his group inside it to the bottom of the hill. However, the road in front of him did not appear to sway, nor did he feel at all dizzy. He decided to drive carefully on for as long as he felt no worse.

The Park was quite near at last. He was seeing it from above, looking down even on the high dome of the Pleasure Palace. The spirally twisted red-and-white stripes were reassuringly steady, and so was the minaret-like top of a helter-skelter tower just beyond the Palace, and so were the hugely elongated grey neck and disproportionately small head of a perhaps life-size model of a dinosaur whose body was hidden behind low trees beyond the helter-skelter. He began to feel safer, almost as if he had already brought the car to within a few hundred yards of the turnstiles at the Park entrance. But he remembered that in the road ahead there was a steep double zigzag he would have to steer the car down before it would be on the same level as the entrance. Surprisingly soon the road began to dip and in a moment the car was on the zigzag and more surprisingly still he had so little doubt of his ability to steer successfully that he even accelerated slightly when rounding the zigzag's final bend.

He brought the car safely to a stop in one of the few remaining empty spaces at the far end of the large asphalt-surfaced car-park opposite the turnstiles. He quickly opened the door beside his driving seat with the intention of going round immediately to open the other three doors for his disabled passengers. At the instant when he stood fully upright after leaving his seat he felt the same kind of preliminary giddiness that had come upon him this morning just before he had fallen strengthlessly backwards flat on to the carpeted bedroom floor; but now a panic fear of hitting the back of his head on the hard ground surged up in him and gave him the strength to remain standing. He managed to walk round the bonnet of the car with hardly any unsteadiness, though he felt an extreme acceleration in the beating of his heart. Fortunately only one of his passengers needed to be helped to get out of the car, Miss Bilston, whose legs were abnormally short, and he found he could lift her without difficulty gently down from the front seat. The others – Miss Dover, who had a heart condition, Mr Unwin, a sufferer from Parkinson's disease, Mrs Unwin with rheumatoid arthritis – though they were slow in getting out (Mrs Unwin slid out backwards) – did not expect or want a steadying hand from Leslie; and Willie Tyler, giving no outward sign of disability at all, was almost running as he came round the car from the driver's door, which he could reach because the front seat was a long undivided one made for three people including the driver. Soon they were all walking at the pace of the slowest, Miss Bilston, towards the turnstiles across the asphalt, and Leslie succeeded in willing himself to begin talking with simulated enthusiasm about the Scenic Railway they would be going on this afternoon. He told them he was greatly looking forward to it, as he knew it had been wonderfully changed since he had last been on it ten years before and it was now said to be the most remarkable of its kind anywhere in the world. Wanting to make amends to them for his long silence during the drive he persevered in forcing himself to be cheerfully talkative until, with a little relief, he was aware of having arrived within a few yards of the entrance of the Happiland Park, inside which he would before long be meeting other drivers for the organisation who would already have got there with their groups, and his responsibility for his own group would be shared, or if necessary the main organiser, Nigel Crowbridge, could take over from him altogether.

Under the barkless and highly varnished criss-crossing tree branches of the big rustic entrance arch Crowbridge was standing near the thatch-roofed hut from which the turnstiles were controlled. At the sight of him, unshakily upright in spite of being in his middle eighties, Leslie knew it would not be easy to complain to him of feeling shaky himself, and it would be even less easy to suggest to him that some of the other drivers should be asked to make room in their cars for Mr and Mrs Unwin and Miss Dover and Miss Bilston and Willie when the time came to take all the disabled people home again. But though Leslie did not feel unsteady on his feet now, this might be only because fear of falling was still keeping him tensely upright; and for how much longer would his fear, even if it were to rise to the level of panic again, have power to suppress the extreme vertigo that might be lurking in him? He might be more seriously unwell than he had yet suspected. He would be guilty of criminal irresponsibility if, out of shame at the thought of having to reveal his weakness to Crowbridge, he failed to tell him anything about it and took the risk of driving his own group back to their homes. Undoubtedly the revelation would come as a shock to Crowbridge, who looked all too pleased to see Leslie's group approaching (perhaps they were late and he'd been wondering whether Leslie's car had broken down). 'The Scenic Train is waiting for you in the station', he told them as he welcomingly waved them on through the turnstile nearest to the hut – he must have arranged beforehand that they, and Leslie, should go through without having to buy entrance tickets – and while Crowbridge stayed behind at the hut to pay the ticket man there Leslie's group began to move off on their own, Mrs Unwin holding Miss Bilston's hand, towards the glass-roofed and glass-walled station less than a hundred yards away across a gravelled open space. Leslie lingered until Crowbridge joined him, but before he could bring himself to say anything about his giddiness Crowbridge said,

'A ride on the Scenic Railway is the ideal amusement for them here – quite exciting without being at all bumpy or alarming.'

He spoke in the confidential tone of one public school man talking to another about people he did not regard as their social equals. For a moment this antagonised Leslie so acutely that it could have spurred him to say immediately that he wouldn't be driving his disabled group back home today, but he noticed that Willie Tyler had lagged behind the others and was still within earshot. He did not want Willie to hear something which could spoil his enjoyment of the Happiland Park from the start.

The reason for Willie's lagging behind was most probably that he was keen to continue being near Leslie, who unlike any of the other drivers for the organisation, including Crowbridge, did not treat him as a compulsive fibber to be tolerantly humoured but accepted his exaggerations and inventions with something of the kind of interest and willing suspension of disbelief required by serious works of fiction. Leslie decided, as he and Crowbridge caught up with Willie on their way to the Scenic Train, that he would not tell Crowbridge about his giddiness till after the whole party of the disabled people and their drivers had finished the 'high tea' Crowbridge had ordered for them at the terminus restaurant, and that he would make the telling easier by offering to pay for a taxi to take his own group back to their homes. But even before he and Crowbridge and Willie caught up with the rest of his group the slight feeling of relief his decision gave him was followed by a sudden new premonitory dizziness which in turn, almost instantly, was countered by a powerful renewal of fear in him. He wasn't diverted at all from this fear when he saw, just outside the station and jutting up from the steep valley beyond, the head and shoulders of a gigantic glossily coloured plastic effigy of a famous film-cartoon character, a sailorman whose name Leslie could not at once remember, with puckered-up cheeks indicating a hidden clenching of toothless gums and with a short-stemmed clay pipe stuffed so far into his pursed-up mouth that the clay bowl almost touched his bulbous nose – an effigy which helped to intensify Leslie's fear because in its hugeness it was strange enough to have been an hallucination produced by a dizzy derangement of his eyesight, though he was as sure as he could be that it was objectively real. And when he came with Crowbridge and Willie and the rest of his group into the station, the green-tailed and vermilion-mouthed dragon train waiting at the platform seemed similarly sinister.

The small roofless darkly shiny carriages, linked closely together like green-painted vertebrae of a monstrous snake, were mostly occupied already by other disabled groups in the organisation, and while Crowbridge went forward to speak to and sit beside one of the other drivers – Colonel Disley – Leslie's group got into the last carriage in the train. When Leslie carefully lifted Miss Bilston on to a seat beside Mrs Unwin he was again conscious of the violent beating of his heart, and this did not at once become any less violent after he had quickly sat down next to Willie who had chosen to sit with an empty seat beside him no doubt in the hope that Leslie would take it.

Their seats were the rearmost ones in the train. The tail of the dragon, with what appeared to be a large metal arrowhead at the tip of it, curved up over their heads from behind them. Willie was pointing up at this and trying to say something, but he was unable to enunciate a single word. He got no help from Leslie who, soon after sitting down securely on this seat that had a high outer side designed presumably to hinder anyone from falling out of the carriage accidentally, felt a new dread which for a while distracted his attention from everything other than itself. It supplanted his fear of falling and it had misery in it combined with a different fear. It was a dread that he might not succeed in avoiding attacks of vertigo after today merely by giving up his work for the organisation, and that the extra pressure he had been putting on himself for two months now might already have done him an injury severe and lasting enough to force him to give up his political activities too. At a time when the anti-capitalist cause, which for so many years had been more important to him and Lana than anything else in their lives, was at its lowest ebb yet in the advanced capitalist countries of the world and needed the utmost help its supporters could give it, he had in all probability made himself permanently useless to it. He was so deeply depressed by this thought that he lost all awareness of Willie sitting beside him, and he hardly noticed the train starting to move and the scenery coming into view just outside the station.

Or was it the scenery, not the train, that was moving? Certainly he felt a vibration which could have been transmitted to his uncushioned wooden seat from wheels turning on rails beneath the carriage. But the high grass alongside the track was passing at a speed impossible for the train itself to have achieved so soon, except at a rate of acceleration that would have brought excessive discomfort to its passengers. Yes, relatively to the track, the scenery was moving – and so was the train, but much more slowly – and the grass beside the track was moving faster than the more distant scenery, though this too seemed to move less slowly backwards than the train moved forwards. The difference in speed between the passing of the trackside grass and of the blueish romantic-looking hills in the background must have been intended by the designer of the railway to create an illusion that the hills were at a distance of many miles from the train, whereas actually they were unlikely to be as much as twenty yards away and had possibly been painted on the canvas of a long high horizontal backdrop which was kept moving by vertical rollers revolving behind it. How ridiculous the blueish hills seemed, and how inferior to the reality they were hiding – the real tree'd valley descending steeply to the sea. For a while he stared at the backward moving artificial scenery – though without clearly focusing it, because now almost everything in his immediate surroundings was becoming excluded from his consciousness again, this time by a misery which was less about the unlikelihood of his being able to continue his political activities than about the present state of the cause whose triumph he and Lana had once so confidently hoped would extend all over the world before they died. Yet, as he half-unseeingly stared, an imaginary scene based partly on the actual artificial one though much more alerting and substantial-seeming became visible in his mind.

The blueish hills were replaced by a wide mud-coloured treeless and grassless landscape that was sloping downwards from the fore ground on the right and rising again to a horizon not less than a mile away in the background on the left, and two parallel military trenches that had been dug a hundred yards or so apart went down the slope and then up to and over the horizon. He remained well aware that none of this was in actuality being shown by the moving backdrop he stared towards, but the imagined scene was incomparably more vivid and significant than the actual external one which was still visible to him, though faintly, beneath it. From along the whole viewable length of the trenches unarmed soldiers began to emerge, only a few at first but soon many, who met in the no-man's-land between the trenches. He was seeing the beginning of the fraternisation of British and German troops on the first Christmas Day of the First World War, and he was seeing it because it had always been for him and Lana one of the guarantees history had given that the ordinary people of all nations would eventually join together against the rulers in whose interests they had been tricked into killing one another. He watched the British and German soldiers exchange helmets, show family photographs to each other, visit each other's trenches, start playing a game of football in no-man's-land. But a feeling which might have become elation was quickly aborted in him by his foreknowledge, as he watched these men, that the generals on both sides would soon regain control of them and mutual slaughter would be resumed and would be continued through three more Christmases without any further fraternising breaks and that he would live on into and through a Second World War brought about like the First by imperialistic capitalism, which would survive it to prepare for a Third.

However, the misery reviving in him now was checked by his awareness of a change that was coming over the imagined scene. He was still looking at a wide treeless, houseless and hedgeless stretch of land, but here the ground was dark to the point of being black, and instead of trenches there were innumerable parallel plough-furrows in it which reached from the railway uninterruptedly up to the horizon. It was apparently boundless in all directions like the sea, or like a landscape in another world. It was a Ukrainian field he had seen from a train when he had been on a visit to the Soviet Union during the spring of 1932, in ignorance of the famine that had followed the peasants' resistance to Stalin's forced collectivisation policy and before the assassination of Kirov and the beginning of Stalin's pre-Second World War political purges. It had been all the more impressive and exhilarating because he had seen it as a field in a vast country where for the first time anywhere the domination of the capitalist class had been broken and power had been taken over by a government which had proclaimed solidarity with the workers everywhere in the world. But he was seeing it now as a field in a country where great-nation patriotism had for too long been more evident than Leninist internationalism. The thought of this, and of the decline of international working-class support for the Soviet Union that the retreat from Leninism there had both caused and been prolonged by, renewed the misery Leslie had been feeling just before the Christmas Day trenches began to change to the furrows of the ploughed field. That imagined field was fading now, making him aware again of the actual dragon train he seemed to have been travelling in for quite a long while already with Willie beside him, and of the continuously moving artificial scenery showing at present an assemblage of holiday motorcoaches parked under palm trees on a Mediterranean-like seafront, though before long his imagination was once again transforming the scenery.

He was looking at an expanse of rough countryside with low hills gorse-covered except where the slopes had been cleared to make way for vineyards and for groves of olive trees. A motor-coach which came up along a valley road stopped in the foreground. As its passengers got out of it almost the only thing to distinguish them immediately from an ordinary random group of mainly elderly late-summer-holiday tourists was that there were more men among them than women, but he knew that he was seeing in his imagination a party of British veterans of the International Brigade who with a few of their relatives were able at last, after the death of the Spanish fascist dictator Franco, to revisit the Jarama valley where forty years earlier the British battalion had taken part in halting the fascist offensive against the vital road linking Valencia with Madrid, and on the first day of going into action had lost three hundred men out of six hundred. He saw they were singing now as they and the few women with them walked up the valley away from the motorcoach, and in his mind he heard the tune and the words of their song, the words of the original version of the famous Jarama song they had first sung during the three months they had been ordered to stay on in the valley after the fascist offensive had been checked – 'For 'tis here that we wasted our manhood / And most of our old age as well.' They came to a stop in front of a single tree on an open space of higher ground, and standing in a semicircle they sang a verse of the Internationale. One of the men stepped forward towards the tree, then turned to face the rest of the group. He was holding with both his hands a small oblong packet which was tightly sheathed in a covering of thick plastic. He had difficulty in opening the packet but he persisted without awkwardness and drew out a small wooden casket and scattered the ashes it contained. Leslie knew that these were the ashes of a veteran who had wanted to join the others here but had died in England only a few days before their coach tour had begun. The feelings of the veterans watching the scattering of the ashes did not plainly show in their faces – until suddenly a tall man standing at the far side of the semicircle bowed his head and bitterly wept. He was grieving, Leslie knew, not only for the comrade they were commemorating here, nor only for the many comrades who had been killed during the war against fascism in Spain, but also for the cause of working-class internationalism that had suffered a defeat then from which, after more than forty years, it had not yet recovered.

Leslie realised that he too was weeping, and at the same time he was aware that the dragon train in which he was riding was drawing into the terminus station of the Scenic Railway. He was sure that Willie must have seen him weeping, but he hoped that the other four members of his group occupying the seats immediately in front of him had not seen. With difficulty he pretended to be about to sneeze, and bringing out a handkerchief from his pocket as if to blow his nose he wiped his eyes and his cheeks. By the time the train came to a stop at the terminus platform his eyes and cheeks were dry, and he was able to assume a look which he hoped was at least unmiserable if not actually cheerful as he helped Miss Bilston down from her seat in the train. He got the impression that neither she nor Miss Dover nor the Unwins had seen his tears; possibly their attention had been hypnotically held by the artificial scenery they had been staring at. Walking with them along the platform he was surprised to find himself free both from any premonition of vertigo and from the intense fear of falling that had kept him upright on his way to the train. And now he saw something that inexplicably freed him also from the grief he had been feeling in the train.

It was a tree. Not one depicted on the artificial scenery nor one created by his imagination but a real tree rooted in the steep slope of the real valley and visible through the high glass side-wall of the station. He saw it only for a moment as he followed his own group and the other disabled groups out of the station on their way to the Aviary, famous especially for its birds of prey, which was to be the first of several other exciting though not too alarming or physically risky amusements they were to be treated to before they had their 'high tea' at the terminus restaurant. He could not understand why the tree had affected him in the way it had, and a need to understand this grew strong in him before he reached the entrance to the Aviary, where Colonel Disley stood waiting for him. Broadly short, hatless, large-spectacled and with a face like Rudyard Kipling's though there was nothing else literary about him (Leslie had discovered that he had never heard of D. H. Lawrence), Disley was about to say something to Leslie, who however got in first with, 'Do you mind keeping an eye on my group for a short while? I want to go and pay a visit back at the station.' Leslie hadn't noticed whether or not there was a Gents at the station but if there wasn't Disley luckily didn't seem to know there wasn't. 'See you later,' he said, 'and perhaps you'll drop in at my house for a drink when this jaunt's over.' Leslie, putting on a look of urgency which he hoped would be taken as a convincing excuse for his not answering this invitation, hurried away from Disley in the direction of the station.

The tree was a sycamore, autumnal, with the wings of its seeds showing clearly among its not yet fallen leaves, a very tall tree rising from a projecting grassy ledge many feet below in the steeply sloping side of the valley and reaching up as high as the top of the glass roof of the glass-walled terminus. It reminded him of a tree that had been outside the railway station of his home town, the town where he had been born, though the tree there had not been a sycamore but an ash and had grown out of the side of the high embankment on which the station had been built. At the bottom of the embankment a road had led to a taxi-cab rank, whereas at the bottom of the valley here and almost directly below the sycamore was a pond, a surprisingly large one with reeds growing round it and with birds – could they be ducks? – swimming on it. Its water was too high above sea-level to be sea water and must have accumulated gradually in an impermeable hollow created by a landslide some while ago. He remembered the reedy pond in the public park of his home town. He noticed quite near the terminus entrance a narrow path leading down along the side of the valley to the foot of the sycamore and then curving on down to the pond. He decided to go a little way along this path to get a better view of the pond. He felt sure that neither Disley nor Crowbridge would take it amiss if he left his group in their charge rather longer than he had given Disley to expect.

Disley, who was greatly interested in birds of prey, did not notice that Leslie at least ten minutes after leaving him to 'pay a visit' at the station had not yet returned; but Willie did notice, and his curiosity about what Leslie might be doing overcame the keen interest he too had in condors and vultures and eagles. He was able to walk out of the Aviary without being immediately missed by Disley or Crowbridge or by any of his disabled friends – somewhat like a little boy who gets lost in a zoo when the attention of his parents and his siblings is monopolised for a moment too long by the antics of one of the animals – though Willie was away for so short a time that only the sight of him running as fast as he was capable of when he came in again through the Aviary entrance made Disley aware that he had been away at all.

He was desperately trying to say something, and totally failing. Disley, who prided himself on his skill in helping Willie to talk, experimentally suggested various words to him to get him started, such as 'money', 'pocket', 'train', but Willie shook his head each time until Disley said 'Mr Brellis', and then he vigorously nodded. Eventually Disley got out of him that Mr Brellis was paddling, not in the sea but in a pond with ducks on it, and that the pond was half-way down the side of the valley. Disley repeated this story, with an ill-disguised wink, to Crowbridge who had come up to him to propose that they should take the party on to see the Smugglers' Cave and also the Aquarium before taking them to the restaurant. Then Disley said to Willie, 'Mr Brellis would have had to look pretty slippy to get down there in the short time since he was with us here.' 'He did slip,' Willie said, enunciating the words very clearly. Disley and Crowbridge exchanged inconspicuous smiles. But they didn't feel inclined to go on humouring Willie, who was unsuccessfully and agonisingly trying to add something to his story.

Leslie knew that he did slip, at the top of the path leading downwards to the foot of the sycamore. With astonishing velocity he sat down on a hard surface somewhere below the path, jarring his spine. His legs dangled into a softness as of high grass. He was surprised to feel no pain, and the ease with which he was able after a minute or two to stand up again seemed to prove that he had not injured himself at all. On the contrary he felt strangely invigorated, and not only physically. His imagination became even more strongly alive than when he had watched the artificial scenery from the dragon train, and the scene he began to imagine now was so vivid that it completely replaced in his consciousness the real sycamore and the real valley.

• • •

HE WAS STANDING at the top of a long covered footway that sloped down from the station platform-exit towards the side road leading leftward to the taxi-cab rank and rightward to the main street of his home town. The unwalled gaps between the iron pillars that upheld the curved roof over the footway gave a high clear view of the brewery tower and the church spire and even of the short bridge under which flowed (though he couldn't yet see it) the small river whose course through the town, whether briefly in the open or more often concealed in culverts, he remembered so well that he could almost have sketched a rapid map of it in his notebook as he stood here now. But sketching anything at all would have been made impossible for him by his emotion at the sight of his home town.

He felt gladness, and he felt sorrow, and above all he felt love – not only his own love for this town he had been too long away from but its love (which seemed to emanate from everything he saw now) for him. Yet when he walked down the footway and came out on to the side road, the love he felt began to have anxiety in it. He was afraid that during all the years since he had last been here the town might have changed too much for him to find his way back to those places he most of all needed to revisit.

For a while nothing appeared unfamiliar to him. He crossed the main street near where it went beneath the brown brick railway bridge, and after turning away from the bridge to walk along the pavement towards the town centre he soon reached Southern Road, which ran parallel to the railway and looked entirely unchanged, with the trees all along both sides of it and even up to the far end of it easily recognisable as London planes by the light-coloured patches where the bark had flaked off from their trunks. The plane trees helped to assure him, as he crossed the entrance to Southern Road and walked on along the main street, that he was taking the right route to find what he first of all wanted to find, and the assurance they gave him was strengthened as he passed the house of Dr Woodcote and the old Corn Exchange building, which were exactly where they used to be. For a moment he was alarmed when, staring ahead along the main street towards the town centre, he discovered that the market-place which should have been just beyond the crossroads had disappeared and that the whole scene had become unrecognisable. But in the next moment he found he had reached the entrance to the road he had not allowed himself till now to be fully conscious of yearning to reach: Northern Road – and looking along this he could see on one side the wicket gate, as he had privately and romantically named it in his boyhood, which led into a market garden by the back way, and on the opposite side the small convent school which even some Anglican parents (middle-class ones for whom the lower class local Church of England elementary school would have been unthinkable as an alternative) sent their girl children to until they were old enough for the high school – but he could not yet see the house he longed to see.

The street lamps came on soon after he had started walking up Northern Road. He had not realised how late the afternoon had become. There was still no sign of darkness in the air when he passed the convent and reached the first of a group of identical-looking houses, one of which used to be named Braemar. He walked more and more slowly, unable to remember where it had been positioned among the other houses and increasingly apprehensive that he would not be able to recognise it if its name had been changed. But its name had not been changed, was inscribed just as formerly in gilded cursive lettering on the glass above its front door. He dared to stop soon after having very slowly passed the house, and then he turned back and stopped again, this time within a few paces of the gate which he would have to open if he were to decide to walk up the short tiled path to the door.

He stood looking towards the bay window of the front sitting-room. The curtains had not yet been drawn across nor had the light been switched on inside. In his boyhood more than fifty years before he would never have had the courage even to linger for a moment or two here, far less to stand staring as he was now. At most he would have walked or more probably bicycled slowly past the house – but not so slowly that his slowness would have been obvious – hoping that he might get at least a glimpse of Isabelle, or even that she might see him passing, though he was afraid this could make her think worse rather than better of him if he appeared to her to be merely on his way along Northern Road to somewhere else. He was never able to overcome the awed timidity that was caused by the very intensity of his love for her and led him at last to write her the letter which put an end for ever to his hope of being loved by her in return. Standing here near the gate outside her house this evening half a century afterwards he could not forget the final shameful fortnight that had begun when he had dared to post to her, anonymously, a book of poems by Rupert Brooke, bound in brown suede leather. Within a few days this had brought him a brief letter from her saying, sarcastically as it seemed to him, that someone had sent her a beautiful book but unfortunately had 'omitted to enclose their name'. He had written her a panicking answer improbably explaining that he had sent her the book because he had thought she had sent him one but he had realised later that the book he had received must have come from Mr Hobson, an old friend of his family. He never saw or heard from her again. Yet now as he continued staring at the window the memory of this unhappy ending became incomparably less important to him than the scene his imagination soon took him to see inside the room: Isabelle smiling with the lit candles of the Christmas tree behind her when he had arrived for the party where he had met her again for the first time since their childhood at kindergarten together ten years earlier, and before the evening of dancing had been over he had known he was utterly in love with her. How insignificant his miserable timidity was made to seem now by that remembered happiness.

He took a step towards the front gate. He hadn't the least expectation that Isabelle would still be living in this house. Yet if he were to open the gate and go up the path and ring the front door bell, someone who knew something about her might come to the door. He did not open the gate. He remembered that her house had not been the ultimate destination he had aimed to reach when he had set out from the station into the town. He must move on. He could come back here later, perhaps tomorrow. The evening was getting darker, and though he was confident as he began walking again that he was taking the right route, he wanted to see clearly any changes that might have been made to the houses that had once been familiar to him along it. He came to the end of Northern Road and saw on the far side of the T-junction there a large square-shaped yellow-brick house recognisable to him immediately as the one where Mr Hobson had lived. He walked towards it across a road which meant more to him than any other in this town - Junction Road, at the end of which his own home had been. In the lower rooms of Mr Hobson's house the lights were on. It might not be impossible, he thought, that in these times when more people than formerly reached a very advanced age Mr Hobson was still alive. Leslie did not stop to stare at the windows here but walking on he remembered Mr Hobson's offer to him long ago of a job which could have led eventually to a partnership in Mr Hobson's prosperous and by bourgeois standards reputable firm. If he had accepted that offer he might have become a success, highly respected in the town, though even supposing the prospect of that success might have persuaded Isabelle to forgive him and to marry him he was as certain still as he had been then that he would have found such a job unbearable. And Isabelle could never have been what Lana had been to him. But as he continued walking he thought with gratitude and warmth of Mr Hobson who, childless, had at one time seemed to regard him almost as a son and had genuinely wanted to help him.

FROM THE MOMENT when he got a first glimpse of his own home ahead at the corner of Junction Road he could no longer think of

Mr Hobson or even of Isabelle. Nor could he think about his home: he could only feel, and his feeling was of fear as well as of yearning. He was not, or would not let himself be, fully aware of what he was afraid of. The exterior of the house, so far as he could see by the light of nearby street lamps when he reached the corner of the road, had suffered no hideous change since he had last seen it. The virginia creeper at its red autumnal best now was still thick on the house walls, and where the wide gravel path leading from the double front gate to the front door narrowed as it went on beyond the bow-window of the drawing-room he saw that the two privet hedges were still densely there hiding the sunken garden which the path zigzaggingly reached through the gap between their overlapping ends. How often in his childhood he had trickily steered his pedal motorcar at speed down that zigzag and how often the chain had slipped off the cogs as he had struggled to pedal it up again. The remembrance helped him temporarily to forget his fear as he opened the customarily used right-hand half of the double gate − (had the other half ever been used?) − and went along the very short gravel 'drive' to the front door. But when he stood in the porch and was facing the door his fear returned.

The light visible through the thick wavy semi-transparent glass panels of the door was as dim almost as it had been during black-out hours in the Second World War (though it had never been really bright even when he had lived here before the war). Like a stranger now he had to press the bell-push beside the door instead of being able to let himself into the house with his latch key. He did not hear the bell ring and no one came to the door. He found just above the door-handle the familiar unpolished bronze knocker, shaped like the head of an Egyptian pharaoh, blacker than ever, and he knocked twice with this, not too loudly. Soon he saw someone moving slowly in the hall who loomed up towards the glass panels and at last reached the door. He did not instantly recognise his mother when she opened the door, because he had hardly had the remotest hope that she would still be here, but she knew him at once. 'Oh Leslie,' she said, and she put her arms round his shoulders and kissed him. 'I'm so glad.'

'I wish I could have let you know beforehand that I would be coming,' he said.

She seemed not to hear this. 'I'm so glad,' she said again, and then she called out into the hall, 'Arthur, it's Leslie.'

His father came out from the morning-room at the back of the hall. He shook hands with Leslie. Long ago Leslie had felt hurt that after he had reached the age of thirteen his father when welcoming him home from boarding-school or saying goodbye at the end of the holidays had taken to shaking hands with him instead of kissing him, but the warmth of his father's handshake now did away finally with Leslie's fear. His parents were both of them not only still alive but looked not so very much older than when he had last seen them.

'You are just in time for tea,' his mother said, leading the way into the large room which she had long ago named the south room. The light here was a little less dim than in the hall. There was a teapot covered with a knitted woollen cosy on the antique small round table in the middle of the room. His mother went to the dark oak corner cupboard at the end of the room to fetch an extra teacup and saucer and a plate. He sat down in the brown leather armchair he so well remembered. His father sat down opposite him in an almost identical chair, though with an inflated rubber ring for a cushion just as formerly. Leslie had a feeling of safety such as he believed would not have been possible for him anywhere else than here.

The things he had especially wanted to tell his parents began to seem less urgent as he rested so comfortably in this chair. He must not let himself forget what these things were, however. He wanted to say how sorry he was that because of the work he had been doing he had not been able to come home before today. He wanted to say how sorry he was that he had disappointed them long ago by not taking the job Mr Hobson had offered him, and to explain that he could not have endured it and that the life he had chosen had been the only tolerable one for him. He wanted to admit that this work he had given his best energies to had not been a success, nor had the cause he had worked for, though also he would tell them he had never doubted – and was more convinced than ever – that it would triumph in the end. But why should he risk upsetting his parents by saying any of these things? Their happiness at having him here with them again was so evident. And why should he risk disturbing his own happy drowsiness which was increasing in him every moment as he sat here? 'Home is a place where I am well thought of,' he said to himself as he sank into the comfort of his armchair, as he slid more deeply, more and more deeply, downwards into its safety.

INVESTIGATION AFTER MIDNIGHT

I HAVE WOKEN EARLY, much too early, as I've so often done this winter. For several moments I feel I've had a long refreshing sleep, and I estimate that when I turn my head to look at the glowing ruby-red figures of our bedside digital clock I may see them form, in their awkward rectilinear way, the letters S O S (Elsie and I have each of us had this same brief illusion once or twice during the last few weeks, no doubt because we are both of us more literate than numerate) and I shall then know I have only two hours and twenty-five minutes to go before I reach our habitual getting-up time of half-past seven. But in actuality what the clock-face scaringly shows when I look now is 2 5 0 which I immediately see as numerals and as time, not as letters. I need to make myself believe that having to lie awake for the next five hours and forty minutes wouldn't matter to me in the least. If I can succeed in genuinely believing this I may even increase the likelihood of my falling asleep once more, though also I need to prevent myself from beginning to remember the dream I have just woken from.

Something about it I'm already failing to avoid remembering is that, in spite of the nightmarishness of the events in the dream, I did not want to wake from it. Or perhaps what I really did not want was to wake from the oblivion into which it had intruded like a hostile stranger. Stop thinking about this at once. Stop thinking altogether. Let me repeat to myself again and again the saying I have recently found less ineffective than any of the other would-be hypnotic devices I have been experimenting with to out-manoeuvre insomnia: 'The day is for thinking; the night is for sleeping.' I can think about the dream in the morning, and I can describe it to Elsie at breakfast. But I might forget most of its details by then, and if I did allow myself to remember them now they might not be as great a threat to my chances of sleeping soon as if they remained half-hidden at the back of my mind.

It was daytime and I was downstairs in the hall of a house much like our own present one, except that the hall was lighter than ours because on both sides of the front door were windows we haven't got. Elsie wasn't with me but was possibly somewhere upstairs. From outside the door a noise was approaching which I took as little notice of as we usually took of the many often louder noises made by the contractors who were converting the large next-door house into a residential home for the elderly. We did not doubt they would have liked to drive us out of our house and to reconstruct it as an annexe to their 'home', and they might have succeeded months before if our hearing hadn't become less sensitive than when we were younger. But my sight hadn't detriorated enough to prevent me from seeing, through one of the windows beside the front door, five burly young men advancing, the biggest of them carrying another hardly less big astride on his shoulders. Raucously yelling, the biggest ran full tilt at the door, using the heavy-booted stiffly extended legs of his rider as a battering-ram. The din would have sounded exceptional even to Elsie upstairs − if that's where she was − yet the door didn't give way until the other three, also yelling, had flung themselves several times at it, kicking it with such violence that I assumed their boots must have steel toe-caps. As soon as the two battering-rammers got into the hall the less big one who had been the rider stood up on the shoulders of the bigger and somersaulted over his head to land on the carpeted floor of the hall with the light-footedness of a circus acrobat descending from a trapeze. All five of them then came to stand round me in a ring, their postures seeming relaxed rather than immediately threatening. But someone walked briskly in from outside the house and broke through the ring to stand closely facing me. Unlike the others, all of them in overalls, he wore a suit and I recognised him as the contracting firm's boss who a week or two previously had noticed my look of hate as I had watched him get out of his expensive Executive car in front of our house. Peering at me now through the short pale lashes of half-closed eyes, he said with an ironic leer,

'Mr Alan Sebrill, I think.'

He evidently knew that this name I had been going under ever since Elsie and I had retired here was not my real one but a literary pseudonym.

'And who are you?' I asked, trying to give no sign of finding any meaning in his leer other than that he intended it to be aggressively insolent.

He contemptuously ignored my question, and turning to the men around us he nodded towards the staircase at the back of the hall. Without even glancing at me he walked out of the house, while four of the men ran towards the stairs. I felt fear for Elsie, until suddenly I remembered that before the men had arrived she had gone into the kitchen, not upstairs. I anxiously hoped she would have got out of the house and through the gate at the end of the garden to give the alarm in the town. I turned angrily to the man who had stayed beside me in the hall, the biggest of the men, and I asked,

'What are you doing here?'

'Just clearing up,' he said.

He spoke in a high-pitched falsetto voice, his arching eyebrows above his wide-opened eyes causing deep wrinkles to ripple upwards over his forehead till they reached his scalp and made the bristles of his close-cropped hair undulate slightly, while his mouth spread out in a grin like a circus clown's nearly from ear to ear.

'I must ask you to leave the house at once,' I said.

I had become convinced that this house, in spite of a few inexplicable differences, was our own home which we had been living in for years.

His grin and his wrinkles vanished and he said in a hard unartificial voice,

'You would do better to keep your mouth shut. There are some real bastards with me here and I can't answer for what they might do if they heard that kind of language from you.'

He moved closer to me, and after an astonishingly short while the four men began coming rapidly down the stairs, the first man carrying our pair of antique cane-bottomed bedroom chairs, one of which was upended on the other and piled with pillows, the second man balancing our latex double mattress over his head and shoulders, the third hugging to his chest our mahogany bedside cabinet with the digital clock on top of it, the fourth supporting on his interdigitated hands a towering heap of my clothes of all kinds which he held out upright in front of him like a juggler as he bounded down the stairs and followed the others through the front door into the front garden, where they dumped their burdens before hurrying back into the hall and up the stairs again.

'Are they taking absolutely everything, even my clothes?' I protestingly asked the man beside me who now stood so near that he breathed down into my face as he answered,

'Naked you came into this world –'

He did not finish the quotation.

I am uncertain whether the arrival of two women wearing hospital nurses' uniforms was what happened next, or whether I am involuntarily creating them as I lie awake trying to remember my dream. They haven't come in through the front door but from somewhere at the back of the hall, I hope not from the kitchen where they might have found Elsie. I recognise, without knowing how, that their bright blue uniforms are bogus and are meant to deceive persons ignorant of the type of uniform an authentically qualified nurse would wear. They are coming straight towards me – strongly built, cold-faced women who separate after they reach me, one of them taking hold of my right arm, the other of my left. They begin to pull off my jacket. I struggle against their efforts to undress me, but the woman on my right, the older of the two, grips and gives a quick twist to my genitals, and as I double up with pain they pull off my trousers from behind. I am incapable of resisting them while they take off the rest of my clothes. The older says to the younger,

'It's started up my rheumatic shoulder again. I wish we'd had time to do him softer, like we do the old men in the home, don't we Sharlene?'

'Yes, they responds well to that.' Sharlene speaks the word 'responds' as though it doesn't come naturally to her but has been taught to her by her employer.

Without having spoken to me directly at all they pick up my clothes and carry them to the open front door which, battered though it is, they manage to shut as they go out of the house, and I'm left standing naked alone in the hall.

Immediately after they've gone several men, presumably the same who went out before them, start nailing up plywood boards against the windows and the door from outside. Soon no light is getting into the hall except through the semicircular window like a setting sun above the door. I go to the nearest electric switch on the wall and when I press it the bulb does not come alight in the lantern hanging from the hall ceiling. I go to the telephone on the small table near the door and I find that the flex has been cut away and removed. Unless Elsie has escaped no help can be expected from outside. The plywood boards which I don't doubt have been nailed up over all the ground floor windows and outer doors by now won't arouse suspicion in any of the passers-by. Everyone will think that this house is to be included in the residential home under construction next door and that the boards are intended by the contractors to keep thieves and vandals out meanwhile. Elsie has almost certainly not escaped but has been trapped somehere in the house: the contractors would not have been likely to board it up if they'd found she wasn't here and could give the alarm. We are to be abandoned to starve here and they could bury our bodies undiscoverably in thick concrete under the floor of the cellar. I go towards the kitchen in fear to look for her. I never reach the kitchen. I decide that my dream, which I'm increasingly sure is no longer being truly remembered by me but has become a fake produced by my all too wide-awake imagination, must be dismissed totally from my mind if I am to have any hope of going to sleep again.

But I'm not succeeding in preventing myself from feeling a need to find out what caused me to have this particular dream, and already I've begun to remember the news Elsie came back with after shopping yesterday morning. Yet another house in the town had just become a privately run old people's home, she told me, and this time it was the large house next door to us which after the death of our neighbour Reg Yalden had been taken over by a buyer we'd not yet met who had been having builders in for some while making alterations to it. She had read a notice pinned up beside its front door which said that the home was for the elderly and mentally infirm, and she had gone in to ask the proprietor whether this meant that it was for the mentally infirm elderly or that the elderly would be mixed with the mentally infirm, perhaps of all ages. Not seeming to detect irony or indignation in her inquiry, though he had seemed surprised by it, he had assured her that the elderly who were not mentally infirm would be kept quite separate from the rest. 'How ghastly it would be,' I said to her, 'if whichever of us survived the other became physically unable to cope alone, and while still perfectly sane had to go into a residential home of that type.'

'I wouldn't stay sane for long,' she said. 'But to be fair to this proprietor, it may be quite true that his inmates who are not suffering from senile dementia or teenage schizophrenia will be kept apart from those who are.'

'And those who are will be half-starved,' I said. 'And so will those who aren't.'

'They could be, but some of these homes are well run, in spite of being run for private profit, and the very bad ones are probably a minority.'

'I would rather be dead than get into any of them, bad or not.'

'The odds are against either of us ever having to,' she said. 'Most old people in this country even when they are quite alone manage somehow to go on living in their own homes to the end.'

'The big danger for us in this town,' I said, 'is the spreading of these profit-making homes at such a rate that we may wake up one morning to discover that our own house with ourselves inside it has been swallowed up into one of them.'

We both laughed. We have often been able to laugh when talking about what is going to happen to us before the end. Whenever either of us develops yet one more chronic old-age ailment we try to console ourselves with a saying of Elsie's, 'Things could be worse – and they will be.' 'Laughing all the way to the grave,' is another of hers; also 'Planning for senility' and 'Planning for finality'; and before her operation when she had a cyst which might have been found to be malignant she said, 'We must be bloody, bold and resolute.' But we have always known well enough that we would not be able to laugh when worse things did happen to us and that there were people who endured the most dreadful sufferings with a heroism we could never match. And now all at once I'm aware of what the main thing in real life was that caused my dream. I'm also aware that until I have let myself remember it fully I can have no hope of sleeping again tonight.

Yesterday afternoon the narrow lane I always go along at the start of my favourite inland walk was half blocked by an old battered-looking lorry to which three men were bringing out some of the contents from the house of a solitary woman who had died a few weeks before in a private residential home. The men were unlikely to be thieves – the amazingly many mattresses, pillows, bolsters and blankets I watched them pile on to their lorry were too filthy and too worn to be worth stealing – but I could not think they were regular municipal workers or that the lorry was Council property. Perhaps the Council, who for some while had been telling her the house must be sold to pay the proprietor of the home where she had at last been persuaded to spend her nights though not yet her days, had been unable because of its inner almost as much as its outer condition to find a buyer for it, and after her death they were employing cheap 'cowboy' labour to remove her soft furnishings from it to the still unprivatised municipal refuse dump. Or perhaps they had succeeded in selling it, and the buyer was employing these men who might not bother to drive as far as the legal dump to tip out their load. I could be certain only that when finally she had been taken full-time into the home she had ceased to be an obstacle to the sale. And I felt ashamed of my failure to do anything which might have helped her to remain free.

Till lately I hadn't even begun to talk with her and to get to know her, though over the last twenty years I had often seen her in this lane and had early on found out that the yellow brick battlemented Victorian-medieval house, strikingly different from any of the other houses along the lane, was hers and that she lived there by herself. I had noticed it in detail before I had noticed her at all, and already then the pointing had been missing from between many of its bricks, and the corbelled-out windows with their high narrow panes separated by vertical glazing bars had shown only faint streaks of paint on their frames. She too, from the first, had seemed neglected and strange, both because of the way she dressed — with a black straw hat pressed down on to her unevenly cut straight hair and with a slantingly hitched-up skirt below a knitted brown jacket which looked like a bed jacket — and because most often when I saw her she was wheeling a bicycle on the handlebars and front basket of which she precariously held a pile of broken dead branches gathered I supposed from nearby woods. I used to say good afternoon to her, and when she was alone she would acknowledge this with a slight shy smile, but when there was anyone else within sight she appeared not to be aware of my greeting, as though she suspected that other people would think ill of her if they saw her smiling at me. She was not wrong in sensing hostility towards her among at least some of her neighbours. Years ago when I was passing the gate of her front garden I had overheard a brief part of a conversation between two men standing near the gate, one of them commenting, 'She's a very strange woman', and the other adding in emphatic agreement, 'I'll say she is.' And quite recently, soon after she had unsmilingly walked past me on her way back to her house with a bundle of dead branches in her arms, a woman who had been watching her from the garden of one of the other houses came out to me, saying indignantly, 'She has stolen those.' I answered, 'Any of us could become like that one day.' And the woman had given me a look of offended incomprehension before returning to her garden. But it wasn't the unkindness of such neighbours that made Miss Elverstead (whose name I didn't discover till I read a brief news-paper report about her after she died) agree to spend her nights though not her days in the residential home. It was, as she told me when less than a year ago for the first and last time I accompanied her some of the way on her late afternoon walk back from her house to the home, the young boys who had been tormenting her every night.

'All round the house and quite close,' she said. 'Making animal noises, screeching and howling'. 'Were they children from houses in the lane?' I asked. 'I don't know,' she said, her voice becoming vague. 'There are so many more houses than when I came here, and a few years before then mine was the only house anywhere near the lane.' I asked whether she had been in touch with the police about the boys, and she said she had and two policemen had arrived one morning to advise her that the best place for her at nights would be in the home. I would have liked to go on to say I hoped she wouldn't mind my being so personal as to ask her to tell me her name and why she had chosen to live in this house and whether any relatives of hers were still alive; but it was more important for me to make sure of finding out from her, before our walk together reached the point where she would be taking the turning towards the home on the main road and I would go ahead farther into the country, about how she was treated in the home, the attention she got or did not get from the nurses, and the quality, quantity and variety of the food she had there. She told me readily enough that she was given nothing more than a cereal and toast for breakfast, though she seemed reluctant to remember her evening meals, and I soon understood that what she most needed to speak of, and she did speak of it for most of the rest of our walk together, was her fear that one morning her house would be taken from her before she could walk back to it. I felt she would never willingly go full-time into the home and I believed that if she was forced to – which at last she was and I do not yet know how – she would never let herself be persuaded she was there for her own good rather than for the financial convenience of the authorities.

As I lie awake now thinking of her and wishing I had done more for her, I tell myself there are other human beings I can still be of better use to than I was to her, but I realise I may live to be incapable some while before my death of helping anyone else in any way again, and I hope that if I become so useless to others I shall remember her example and try for as long as I can to defend the human being I myself am.

PEOPLE HATE ME

NOBODY HELD IT against Victor Yafford's wife Ada that she didn't even pretend to be sorry when he died. For years she had been telling her friends and acquaintances in this spa town about his ill-treatment of her. None of them doubted that what she told them was true, and those she had not told but who knew him would readily have believed her if she had. He was never well thought of by any of his near neighbours in Belton Street, and at least one of them, Jack Derwent, a prosperous local Master-Builder occupying the detached house next to his own, detested him sufficiently to be glad that he was dead. Only James Pelligrew, a retired civil-servant with a Belton Street home farther from the centre of the town, was neither relieved nor indifferent on hearing of Victor's death.

He did not hear of it till nearly a week after it had happened. Noticing an unusual fragrance as he was passing Victor's house to go shopping in the town, he stopped to peer between the untended overgrown bushes into the front garden. Along one side of it the privet hedge was in full bloom, a disorderly wildness which Victor wouldn't have tolerated if he'd been less seriously ill than he was. James Pelligrew recognised the fragrance with some nostalgia as that of privet blossom, and he remained unmoving for a while to savour it. He was just about to walk on when he was startled by the voice of Ada speaking his name.

He turned to her and saw that she was smiling. She had been shopping in the town and carried a loaded wicker-work basket.

He said, 'I hope you will forgive me for not having called in to see you yet this week. I'm afraid I have no excuse. How is Mr Yafford today?'

'He is no longer with us,' she said.

Although Pelligrew had known that Victor could not last much longer, the news came as an unexpected shock to him. He sincerely said, 'Oh I am so sorry to hear that.'

'He died four days ago. The funeral service was at St Saviour's yesterday. There wasn't a wet eye among any of us there.'

Pelligrew could not think what to say to this.

She went on, 'I would be a hypocrite if I didn't admit I feel nothing but relief now that he is dead.'

Pelligrew thought of something he could ask her: 'Will you still be living in this house?'

'I can't afford to keep it up,' she said. 'In his last years he deliberately spent most of his money so that I should inherit as little of it as possible. I shall go and stay with my sister and her husband – unfortunately this will have to be at their expense, though I know they will be glad to help me. I shall stay with them till I can get a job and can earn my own living.'

'If there is anything at all I can do for you please tell me,' Pelligrew said.

'That is very kind of you.' The grateful smile she gave him made him aware, not for the first time, how beautiful her face still was. He had more than once wondered why she'd chosen to marry a man like Victor Yafford who in any case was twenty years older than she was, and the thought had come to Pelligrew that he wanted a housekeeper and that when Victor died he might ask her whether she would consider becoming a housekeeper-companion in his own house. After all, the difference in ages between him and her was not great – he was just over sixty-five and he reckoned she could not be much less than sixty. Also she was intelligent and amiable besides being good-looking. He had an impulse to make her an offer now, at this moment, but he was inhibited both by a feeling that it was too soon after Victor's death and by his own habitual cautiousness, so he said to her as pleasantly as he could:

'Well, I suppose I must go and do my shopping. Can I come to see you again before too long?'

'Yes,' she said, giving him the warmest of smiles.

Smiling also, he lifted his hand slightly to wave goodbye. As he walked on, she was abruptly displaced from his mind by a return of the genuine grief he had unexpectingly felt when she had told him Victor Yafford was dead. How could he feel this grief, knowing as he did what a repellent man Yafford at his worst had been? Pelligrew remembered in particular the summer during which Ada, finding Yafford's treatment of her unbearable at last, left him and went to stay with her sister who was married to a radiologist.

One warm morning as Pelligrew was returning past Yafford's house from the town, Yafford in the garden called out to him, 'Can you spare me a minute or two?'

'Of course,' Pelligrew said; and Yafford, looking morose, opened the garden gate for him and shut it again before leading him on to the lawn.

'Yesterday my wife left me,' Yafford said. 'She went out with her shopping basket in a normal way, but I thought she was taking a long time to come back, and I began to be suspicious, though when I looked into her bedroom upstairs I discovered that none of those things which ladies use had been removed from her dressing-table, and the clothes she kept in her wardrobe were still hanging there.'

'Do you know where she has gone?' Pelligrew asked.

'I don't doubt she's gone to her sister.' There was a bitter harshness in Yafford's use of the word 'sister'. He did not mention that the sister had married a radiologist who was a black man, but Pelligrew had been told by Ada that when Yafford heard of this he ordered Ada never to invite her sister into his house again. Pelligrew guessed that Yafford's reason for not explaining why he hated the sister was his awareness of Pelligrew's disapproval of racism. Yafford did not want to appear in a bad light to him.'

'What are you going to do now?' Pelligrew asked.

'I have got in touch with the Vicar of St Saviour's,' Yafford said. 'It was he who married us and it is up to him to persuade her that it is her Christian duty not to desert her husband.' He became vehement, 'I would never have chosen a church wedding if I hadn't thought that it would bind her more securely to me.'

Pelligrew said nothing.

'I am not the only husband in Belton Street to have been deserted by his wife recently,' Yafford said. 'Mr Veale's wife spilt a cup of tea over him the other day as she handed it to him at the breakfast table. Then he gave her the fireman's chop, and she walked out on him.'

'What is the fireman's chop?' Pelligrew asked.

Yafford clasped his hands together and made a downward chopping movement with them. He explained, 'That's what firemen do when people they are trying to rescue get panicky – hit them on the back of the neck.'

Pelligrew began to feel he'd had enough of Yafford for the present. He said, 'Forgive me, Victor, but I shall have to take this load of shopping back to my house now and get myself some lunch.'

'I hope I shall see you again quite soon,' Yafford said, giving Pelligrew a strangely contrite look.

'Yes,' Pelligrew said; then walking away from him he thought, 'Yafford has realised that the way he has just been speaking to me might lower my opinion of him, and he regrets it. This is why I can't really dislike him, in spite of all that Ada has told me about him. This is why, for the first time ever, I called him Victor just now. But he will never call me James, because he respects me too much.'

When Pelligrew was unloading his shopping-basket in his kitchen he began to think of more things that Ada had told him about Victor. On the second day of her marriage to him she went into the upstairs room which he called his study to have a look round it while he was out in the garden, but somehow he became aware of what she was doing and hurried up the stairs to say very sharply to her that she must never open the door of that room again.

'What did you see inside it?' Pelligrew had asked her. 'Not the corpses of his previous wives, I hope.'

'No,' Ada said with a brief laugh, 'I recognised a lathe and a drill and a vice, and there was a chaos of other tools and bits of metal. I knew that he'd worked for years as a personnel manager for an important engineering firm and that he was keen on making metal models of cars and steam locomotives.'

Later, when Victor had heard of her sister's marriage to a black man he not only banned this sister from his house but he demanded that Ada should take down from the wall of her bedroom all the framed photographs she'd hung there of various other relatives of hers.

A few days afterwards Yafford started his quarrel with Jack Derwent – a neighbourly enough man not known to lose his temper easily.

One of Jack's sons had become a classical jazz enthusiast and had joined a band formed by three other equally enthusiastic young friends of his. On those Saturday evenings when the band gave a performance in the town his friends had begun to make a habit of walking back to his home with him, and sometimes they all stood talking rather loudly outside it. Yafford leant out of his bedroom window once and shouted to them to be quiet, but although this did quieten them temporarily they were almost as loud next time they came.

Yafford after this had called in on Jack Derwent to complain about his son. Derwent momentarily felt inclined to be apologetic, but nettled by the insulting coldness in Yafford's tone he confined himself to saying stiffly, 'I will have a word with him.'

The word was ineffective. The son and his friends were soon too noisy yet again. On the next morning Yafford went to see Derwent once more, but found he had gone out in his car. Between their two houses there was a narrow lane owned in common by the various nearby houses round the back gardens of which it extended. Formerly it had been used on Wednesdays by the municipal dustmen who collected refuse from the domestic dust-bins left out there, though now the bins were left in front of the houses. At the point where the lane turned to go round the back gardens, Jack Derwent, without asking his neighbours whether they minded, had built a garage for his car. Yafford before trying to visit Derwent this morning positioned his own car directly across the entrance of the lane. The youngish woman who opened the door to him, and who was a friend of Ada's without his knowing she was, told him that Mr Derwent had gone out in the car to do some shopping but that she didn't expect him to be out for long. He asked her if she would give him a message as soon as he returned. She said that she would; then a doubt came to him about her reliability, and he said, 'May I ask who you are?'

'I am the cleaning lady here,' she said

He didn't guess that she used the words 'cleaning lady' merely because she knew that this was what he and her employer would call her (though not to her face), but the confidence and correct-ness with which she spoke, in spite of her slightly plebeian accent, disposed him to believe she would pass on his message to Derwent correctly.

'Tell him I that I have left my car across the opening of the lane, and that I shall leave it there until his son stops making a noise out-side the house after midnight. Tell him too that I shall be coming back to see him soon this morning.'

Yafford left her without saying anything more, and went into the garden at the back of his own house to look at the plants growing in his greenhouse.

When Jack Derwent returned from the town with his wife in their car he helped her to carry the shopping into the kitchen without having noticed that Yafford's car was blocking the entrance to the lane. Ada's friend gave him Yafford's message, and she was astounded and scared by the effect it had on him. She had always thought he was an equably-tempered man, but his voice rose wildly out of control as he shouted, 'I'll kill him, I'll kill him, I'll kill him.'

She hurried out of the kitchen and she rang up the police on the phone near the front door.

Luckily a policeman arrived just before Yafford did, and he kept the two men apart while they argued with each other, Derwent in a fury while Yafford was coldly calm. Finally the policeman with some difficulty persuaded Yafford that he should remove his car from blocking the lane, and he warned Derwent, who had now cooled down a little, of the serious consequences that would follow if he ever committed an act of violence against Yafford. Then Yafford walked out of the house and moved his car back into the garage-shed he had built for it in his own front garden.

James Pelligrew, sitting in his kitchen after leaving Yafford, remembered the account Ada had formerly given him of this episode which she had been told of by her friend the cleaning lady, and he reflected that though it was more sensational in its results than any other of all the actions that had caused people to dislike Yafford, it was not the worst of them. Yafford had been right when, with the policeman keeping him and Derwent well apart, he firmly accused Derwent of stealing public property by building himself a garage in the lane. But Yafford's treatment of Ada had always been wrongful and despicable.

On the day when Ada had told Pelligrew of Yafford's death, and he had said he hoped to see her again soon, he walked on into the town to do his usual shopping; then he walked back past Yafford's house without even glancing towards it. But as he carried his shopping basket into the kitchen of his own house he realised that he too had behaved badly to Ada. He must have raised certain expectations in her when he had asked her to let him know if there was anything at all he could do for her, but he felt now that he would never rid himself of the cautiousness which had inhibited him from inviting her to become his housekeeper-companion. When his own wife had died of cancer and his two sons had gone abroad he had learnt to look after himself – though he did employ a middle-aged woman once a week to keep his large house more or less clean – and he decided he would never start an intimate relationship with any woman again, even though he was not yet freed from all feelings of sexual desire. He was aware that his unnatural self-denial was a sign of weakness rather than of strength, and he wished that his career as a Civil Servant hadn't made him so cautious. His thoughts turned with sympathy to dead Victor Yafford, and he wondered whether Victor had wished before he died that he had behaved more kindly to Ada. But this was something that James Pelligrew could never know. Nor could he know whether Victor had once been a pleasanter person, nor – if he had been – why he became what he later on did become.

• • •

VICTOR YAFFORD'S childhood was happy much of the time. Both of his parents, whose only child he was, loved him without treating him over-protectively, and from his early infancy they gladly allowed the two young Wainwright girls Eva and Grace, from the numerous family next door, to take him into their garden to play with the other Wainwright children, who rarely squabbled and were always nice to him, as if he was someone special. Cyril, a Wainwright boy of the same age as he was, soon became his first best friend, and by an arrangement between Victor's and Cyril's parents a governess, Miss Parbury, was engaged to teach the two boys together. But when the boys reached the age of eight Victor's parents sent him to Argyll House, a preparatory boarding school charging high fees, whereas Cyril's parents having so many children could only afford to send him to an ordinary elementary day-school. At Argyll House Victor's homesickness lasted for two or three weeks, and he missed Cyril; then he began to like the school. He was quick to learn what Miss Kirby, who took the lowest form, taught him, and when he got into the second form he came top in the end-of-term exams. He was neither very good nor very bad at games, but though he was not popular in the way that as a really good games player he would have been, he was soon able to recommend himself to most of the boys of his own age by other means. He was inventive, and showed them for instance how they could greatly increase the velocity of their paper darts by giving two extra folds to these and by gluing the folds together so that the points of the darts became extremely sharp. Then by painting a distinctive bright pattern on six of the darts that he had made, he influenced all the other dart makers to paint distinguishing patterns on their own 'flights' of six darts. He also suggested interesting variations in what they did with the clockwork locomotives, tin railway lines, lead soldiers, model field-guns and howitzers, meccano sets, wooden building bricks, which they were allowed to bring with them at the beginning of term from their homes. If at times some of these boys may have felt that Yafford was a bit bossy, they forgot it because he always generously shared with them the sweets and apples his parents sent him. At Argyll House he had followers and he had friends but he had no best friend like Cyril.

He was happy when he was able to meet Cyril again in the holidays. Nothing seemed to have changed between them. They spent whole days together, riding on their bicycles into the countryside, or Victor went to Cyril's home where they used Victor's meccano to make ambitious new models. Also they played cards with the other Wainwright children. But they saw less of each other when the Wainwright father moved with his family to another house a mile or two outside the town.

Cyril went to a grammar school near his new home, and he liked it. Victor, however, was so deeply depressed after his first term at the minor 'public' boarding school called Bessemer chosen for him by his parents that he felt no urge to see Cyril in the holidays, and he was so ashamed of what had happened to him there that he was unable to talk to his parents about it, though his depression was very evident and alarming to them and they pleaded with him to explain why he disliked the school. He was doing well there, they said. His housemaster had sent them a good end-of-term report both on his work and on his games. Victor in terror begged them not to write and tell his housemaster that he was unhappy at the school, and they promised him they would not.

Victor had rightly believed that they would have been horrified by the foul talk he had heard among the boys during his first few weeks at the school. He had wondered how they could have sent him here without first making the fullest inquiries about the kind of place it was. But after those first few weeks he decided he could bear it – until what happened one afternoon in the changing-room. He had been playing football, energetically and not too badly, and he was sitting on his locker taking off his football boots, when an older boy named Steadman who was walking past him suddenly stopped.

'There's an odour here,' Steadman said to him, 'and it's not just the smell of ordinary sweat. It's a real stench, and it comes from you, Yafford. Have you ever realised that you stink when you sweat?'

Victor knew better than to fall into the trap of saying 'No' or 'I don't'. He was sullenly silent.

'What are you going to do about it?' Steadman asked.

Victor did not answer. Steadman looked as though he was on the point of taking a kick at one of Victor's legs. But he checked himself, feeling perhaps that kicking Yafford would be beneath his dignity as a comparatively senior boy.

Steadman turned and walked away from Victor, who then removed the rest of his football clothes and with a towel round him went to the shower at the far end of the room.

Unluckily there were several younger boys in the changing-room who heard what Steadman said to Yafford, and within a day or two Victor was made aware that among the younger boys at least he was becoming generally known by the nickname Smell, which they particularly enjoyed shouting out at him on public occasions such as football matches in which he was playing.

On the second day of his first holidays at home from the school he went out for a walk by himself in the public park. He ignored the famous trees and shrubs of many kinds which the Council of this spa town had been able to afford to plant here. He passed alongside, without giving it a glance, the large artificial lake that was designed to be the main central feature of the park. He reached the downward-sloping wood of dark fir trees that had been planted at the far end. A narrow asphalted path led into this wood, and he walked quickly down it till he reached a point where he thought no one would be likely to see him do what he had come here to do. He took from his pocket a small tin of white enamel paint and a paint-brush, and he painted on the asphalt the words, **PEOPLE HATE ME**. Then he very quickly walked out of the wood and made for the entrance gates of the park. He was fairly confident that no one had seen him go into the wood or come out of it. Today was an ordinary working day and there seemed to be nobody except a few old people about in the park. He had painted those words on the asphalt in order to give real substance to what would otherwise have been simply an idea, and to make sure that he could not forget them. To think of himself as being hated was less humiliating than to recognise that the boys at his school did not hate him – they merely delighted in tormenting him. He believed now, on this second day of his holidays, that his enamelled device indelible beneath the dark fir trees would help to give him the courage he would need on the day when he had to return to the school at the beginning of his second term there. Also it would help him to tell his parents some of his reasons for disliking the school – the foul language for instance (they couldn't very well disapprove of his objecting to that) – and the abusive taunting he got from some of the other boys (though he would avoid the humiliation of going into details about this). Then he would ask his parents to explain why they'd chosen this school for him instead of allowing him to go to Cyril's grammar school where he could have been as happy as Cyril was.

Sitting with his parents in the dining-room at the end of the evening meal on the second day of his holidays, Victor asked why he'd been sent to Bessemer School.

His mother answered him, 'Because it will make a gentleman of you, and this will be an advantage to yourself and to the business you will be working for.'

His father did not mind her implication that he himself was no gentleman. He knew that he was regarded in the town as a tradesman, and his hope was that Victor by becoming a gentleman would raise the status of the business. However he used a different argument in answer to Victor's question.

'We chose Bessemer School for you because it is known to provide a good general education, including Science and practical handicrafts.'

'But it doesn't provide engineering at present,' Victor objected, 'though it's named after a famous engineer.'

'You won't need engineering when you leave the school and come to help me in my ironmongery business.'

Victor's father had set his heart on eventually handing over his business, which was an increasingly successful one, to Victor, his only son. Victor knew this, but he hadn't yet given much thought to the question whether or not he would like to be in his father's business, and it certainly wasn't what he needed to talk to his parents about now.

'Would you have wanted to send me to Bessemer if you had known that the boys there use all kinds of filthy language when they are among themselves and that they are disgustingly insulting to me?'

Victor's parents looked at him in shocked silence. His mother wanted to say, 'Of course we wouldn't have sent you to Bessemer if we'd known this', but she realised that if he refused to go back there next term her hopes of his growing up to be a gentleman could be ended. His father wanted to tell him that what he was experiencing there didn't greatly matter because it would soon be over when he became one of the senior boys, and when in four years' time he left the school he would be all the better equipped to stand up to unscrupulous troublemakers in his adult business life. But the deeply felt puritanism which had been instilled into Victor's father by both of his own parents inhibited him from telling Victor that filthy talk didn't matter much.

After a while Victor broke his parents' silence by saying, 'You needn't worry. This morning when I was in the park I suddenly knew I would be able to cope with Bessemer next term.'

Neither his father nor his mother could succeed in hiding the relief they felt.

'Now you will be having happier days while you are here,' his mother said, 'and you will be able to go and see Cyril.'

His father gave him some very welcome extra pocket money.

Victor's meetings with Cyril were not altogether a success. Their interests had diverged. Cyril was keener on books than on model-making, and the former brother-like intimacy between the two of them did not revive. Victor could not tell him the nickname he had been given at his new school.

At home during the rest of the holidays his father and mother talked with him each day about how he was occupying himself now, but they avoided saying anything about the boys at Bessemer.

FROM THE BEGINNING of his second term onwards Victor faced his tormentors with a stoical endurance which denied them the pleasure they would have got if he had flown into a rage and hit out at them. There were even signs that some of them were becoming bored with taunting him. They continued addressing him as Smell, though not all of them did. Perhaps the few who didn't were never very keen on persecuting him and might conceivably show friendliness towards him later on. One day after playing football he was sitting on his locker in the changing-room, leaning down to take off his boots, when someone stopped in front of him as abruptly as Steadman had done. It was Weston, the head boy of the school.

'You played a very good game today, Yafford,' Weston said.

Victor felt elated by this praise, but (the modern practice of answering a compliment with the words 'Thank you' not having reached English public schools yet) he remained as silent as when Steadman had insulted him.

'I'm sorry about the nickname you have acquired.'

This time Victor was too dreadfully embarrassed to say anything.

'I can imagine how you must feel about it,' Weston went on, sympathetically, 'and I'm afraid there's not much you or I can do about it, though I'll do what I can. The all-important thing is the kind of influence you will let it have on you not only when you become a Prefect here but also after you leave school.' Weston paused to emphasise this last point before going on, 'You can make one of three choices. The first is to treat people you have power over as badly as you have been treated, and I'm sorry to say I believe that this is what men who have had similar experiences to yours at a public school most commonly do. The second is to ignore or be indifferent to the sufferings of others. The third – and unfortunately the least common – is to do everything you can to help the sufferers. Well, my serious advice to you is to adopt the third.'

Weston ended with a friendly smile, and Victor now dared to say, 'Thank you very much.'

Weston went away from him, then walked out of the changing-room.

He never spoke at any length to Victor again. He won an Oxford scholarship and left Bessemer at the end of the term. He was of course highly praised by the Headmaster in a farewell speech, and Victor had discovered during the term that Weston was much admired by the boys because he was outstandingly good both at cricket and at football. This made them forgive him the surprisingly radical opinions he was known to hold, and one or two of the Sixth Formers were said to have been converted to these. Victor never was converted, though for the rest of his life he admired Weston more than anyone else he ever met.

Victor as a Prefect made himself feared and disliked by his juniors, but he did well at his work in the Sixth Form and he could very probably have won a scholarship to a university; however his father, whose health was not good, was keen that he should join the Yafford ironmongery business without delay and get trained there as soon as possible.

Victor made quick progress as a trainee, and he soon realised that he did not like the business and that the prospect of having to spend most of the rest of his life in it was intolerable to him.

One evening as he sat in the dining-room with his mother and father, he said, 'I am very sorry, Father, but I don't feel I can work any longer in the family business.'

'So you are prepared to see it pass into the hands of strangers?' his father angrily asked.

Victor did not answer. His mother said, 'How do you think you are going to earn your living?'

'I shall get a job with an engineering firm,' Victor said.

He quite soon succeeded in getting one. And his parents forgave him, and he was glad to continue living at home.

• • •

THE ENGINEERING FIRM was an important one, and Victor distinguished himself sufficiently there to be offered before long the position of personnel manager, and eventually – though this was after his father died – he became a director of the firm. He stayed on with his mother at home, and out of consideration for her he postponed asking anyone to marry him. Nevertheless he had a sexual relationship with Ivy Westcomb, a middle-aged widow and writer he didn't intend ever to marry or to live with, nor did she intend ever to marry or to live with him.

He first met his future wife Ada when she was a cleaner for his firm after the Second World War, during which she had been paid good wages as a munitions worker in a different firm. When the men came back she lost her job, and this was especially unfortunate for her as her husband had been crippled in the war. She was glad to get the cleaning job with Victor's firm. He was immediately attracted by her, and he was disappointed when he discovered from her that she was already married. She was attractive to him both because of her good looks and because – to his surprise – she was so well-spoken. He gave orders that she was the only cleaner to be permitted to clean his own office.

One morning she asked him if he would be kind enough to allow her a few days' leave from her work. His instant reaction was one of resentment. He knew she must be aware of his feeling for her – he had made it so obvious – and he suspected her of trying to take advantage of it. But his mood quickly changed when she explained that her husband had died in the night.

She returned to work after only four days' leave. Victor showed concern about this, telling her she could have stayed away longer, but she said that she had a sister who was able to help with the arrangements for the funeral, and she asked him if she might have one more morning off in order to attend the funeral service at her church, St Saviour's.

'Of course you can,' Victor readily said.

'When she returned on the following morning he remembered to condole with her about her loss, which he had failed to do previously, and he asked whether the service had been well attended.

'Very well,' she said. 'At least thirty, I should think. Our relatives on both sides, and several of his old friends and/or mine, and quite

EDWARD UPWARD

a number of the acquaintances I gossip with when I go shopping in the town.'

Victor hoped that his face showed no sign of the jealousy this caused him to feel. He warned himself not to reveal the intensity of his interest in her by over-hastily making her the proposition he intended to make. He let many days go by until a morning came when, after she had given him a particularly kind smile, he risked saying, 'There's something I have been wanting to ask you for some time.' He paused, and she looked as if she had no idea of what he was going to ask.

'Would you consider marrying me?'

'Yes, I would,' she frankly answered.

'Will you still consider it when I tell you I shall not be able to marry while my mother is alive? She is old and ailing and without me she would be living alone, except for one old servant.'

'Yes, certainly I shall still consider it.' Ada hoped she was managing to hide her disappointment.

'Will you agree that we should soon announce our engagement?'

'Yes, I will,' she said, surprised and happy.

'What sort of engagement ring would you like?'

'I really don't know; I don't know at all; you must choose for me.'

Next morning he brought her a platinum ring with a diamond in it. 'Does it fit your finger?' he asked her, not offering to try to put it on for her.

'Oh yes it does, it does. Thank you very very much.'

She could see that he would have liked to kiss her, but he did not. He took both her hands in his, and moved his face close to hers; then he said, 'We must behave ourselves in the office.'

THEY DIDN'T COMPLETELY 'misbehave' themselves anywhere till they had got married at St Saviour's some weeks after his mother's death and he had brought Ada back to his house in Belton Street.

During their engagement Ada continued her cleaning and

tidying work – which she spent plenty of time doing every morning in Victor's office while he sat working at his desk. One consequence of this was that she was able to talk to him about her earlier life, and he in return talked to her about his own.

She told him her father and mother had run a newsagent's shop and worked extremely hard with no holidays except the ordinary public ones, and not always those, because their shop sold cigarettes as well as newspapers. They were pleased she did well at school, but neither of them lived to meet Wilf who became her first husband. She left school early so that she could marry him before he was called up into the army. They were able to live together for a few weeks in lodgings. She found she was pregnant after he was sent to France, but she had a miscarriage.

At this point Victor quite anxiously interrupted her. 'There's something I ought to have asked you before we became engaged. Would you still want me for a husband if I told you I don't want to become a father?'

'Yes, I still would,' she said. 'I wouldn't like to run the risk of any further miscarriages.'

'I'm glad of that for both our sakes,' he said.

When Victor told the story of his own earlier life he began by describing in great detail his happy childhood at home and with the Wainwright family next door. He did not feel he had to confide in her about his being called Smell at Bessemer, though he knew now in any case that the objectionable odour he had exuded when sweating was an affliction which had come with puberty and had gone away by the time he was nineteen. He did not feel he needed to tell her either that ever since this experience of his as a junior at Bessemer he had done his best to make himself hateful to people he regarded as his inferiors. The truth was – and he could hardly believe it – that because of his love for Ada and his wish to be equally loved by her (though he regarded her as his inferior) he felt a desire to make himself at least likeable from now on to all the inferiors he had power over.

But not long before his marriage to her there was a change in his feelings towards her. He had left her alone in his office for a while one morning, and when he came back he found she was looking into some papers that were lying on his desk.

'What are you doing?' he asked her.

There was something in his tone which put her on the defensive. 'Naturally I am interested in anything you are interested in,' she said.

'Don't do that again without my permission,' he said.

She was silent, and leaving the papers untidied on his desk she continued the cleaning elsewhere in the office. He sat down again to his work. He too was silent.

At last she spoke. 'I've finished the cleaning for today.' Then she added, 'I'll come here tomorrow at the usual time, shall I?'

'Yes,' he said.

She went out of the door without saying goodbye.

He did not like the spirit of independence he detected in her. He began to wonder seriously whether he ought to go through with his marriage to her. He decided that he must, because he would be acting dishonourably if he didn't, and because he desired her sexually, and because he believed he would be able to control her when she was married to him.

Ada also, as she walked back to her sister's house, had doubts about the marriage. But she too decided she must go through with it, her reasons being that she had given him every cause to expect she would, and that she didn't want to continue to live with her sister – as she'd had to do because the rent of her lodgings had been increased by her landlord since Wilf died.

Next morning both Victor and she tried to behave as if nothing had gone wrong between them on the previous morning. But now there were many things they would never tell each other about. For instance there was Victor's former relationship with Ivy Westcomb, and Ada's friendship with Marty Kelville who had worked in the same munitions firm as she had during the war and whose brother was working in Victor's firm now and could report to Marty on the relations between Victor and his workforce.

Victor and Ada fixed the date for their marriage, and though he was not religious he willingly agreed with her that it should take place in her church, St Saviour's, and that she should make all the necessary arrangements for it with the Vicar.

Not long after her marriage when she was living with Victor in his house he introduced her to James Pelligrew, who was highly regarded by him. She took an immediate liking to Pelligrew, and from the day they first chanced to meet while both were shopping in the town she began to tell him about Victor's treatment of her. The more she got to know him the more she liked him, and the more she wished she had been able to marry him instead of Victor. His sympathy for her gave her greater comfort than the sympathy of anyone else she confided in. But years later when Victor died she was puzzled by the genuine grief Pelligrew showed for him.

• • •

PELLIGREW AS AN administrative grade Civil Servant knew his Greek and Latin classics and could have quoted in Ovid's more concise Latin the aphorism, 'I see and approve of the better course, yet I follow the worse.' It had seemed to him sometimes that these words might be true of Victor. It had also seemed to him from certain signs, such as Victor's unwillingness to appear in a bad light to him, that Victor thought of him as a man who saw the better course and followed it. Or might Pelligrew be flattering himself? Might Victor think of him as a man who had at times perhaps followed the worse, and might this possibility cause Victor to feel friendlier towards him and to try to adopt at times the better course he believed Pelligrew mostly followed?

When Pelligrew had walked on into the town to do his shopping after Ada had told him of Victor's death, and he had returned past her house without even glancing towards it, the thought came to him that Victor during his last few days might have regretted following the worse course.

But the reality was that for as long as Victor remained conscious, and even when he could get upstairs to bed only by crawling on his hands and knees, he was proud that he had made himself hateful to so many people.

Pelligrew's thoughts as he prepared his lunch turned soon from Victor to himself. Shame came over him as he remembered his own cowardly cautiousness and his treatment of Ada. He decided that after his lunch he would go to see her and would ask her to live with him as his housekeeper-companion.

THE WORLD REVOLUTION

I N FRONT OF THE Town Hall not far from Mavis Langley's small detached suburban house a number of demonstrators holding placards fixed to wooden poles stood chatting with one another when she arrived. 'I was afraid I was going to be late,' she said to Kevin Westridge, who during the past few days had been helping her distribute leaflets informing people that a demonstration would be held here this morning.

'No, you are in good time,' Kevin said; 'none of the Councillors have turned up for their meeting yet.'

'I overslept,' she said, 'and I dreamed a horrid dream that I was having the worst attack of influenza I've ever had.' She smiled.

'I woke early,' he said, 'after a nightmare that no one except our own little group with the placards had arrived to demonstrate, and that none of the Councillors took the slightest notice of us as they arrived one by one and walked up the steps to the Town Hall entrance.'

'But actually there are quite a large number of people here,' she said, 'and more seem to be coming at every moment.'

'Yes, and Jack Bailey with several other members of our group have already got themselves up into the public gallery and will be able to demonstrate from there.'

As Kevin delightedly said this, the first Councillor appeared. The demonstrators vehemently shouted the words that were printed on the placards, 'SAVE OUR COTTAGE HOSPITAL' and 'SAVE OUR VILLAGE SCHOOL'.

The Councillor, ignoring the shouts, hurried up the steps and passing under the pillared canopy that fronted the entrance he quickly disappeared into the Hall.

With one exception the Councillors who followed him behaved in the same way. The exception, a florid-cheeked heavily-built middle-aged man, stopped on the steps and turning to face the crowd he spoke loudly enough to make his voice heard above their shouting:

'Don't blame us. Blame the Government cuts.'

He was loudly booed.

A powerfully-voiced person called out: 'We blame you for not having the guts to resist the Government.'

The exceptional Councillor then retired into the Hall as the others had done.

The crowd were continuously increasing and their shouting grew louder and louder. Suddenly Jack Bailey and the other members of the group who had been in the public gallery appeared with policemen behind them violently pushing them out from under the entrance canopy and then down the steps into the crowd, who heartily cheered them and jeered at the police. The shouters, unintimidated, redoubled the volume of the sound which they were determined should continue to penetrate into the Council chamber.

After quite a long while a more important-looking policeman, wearing a different kind of hat – an Inspector's peaked cap instead of a helmet – came out from the door under the canopy and held up his hand to the crowd as if to command silence. They decided to give him a hearing.

'You are wasting your time,' he said; 'the Councillors have left by the exit at the back of the Hall.'

There was a dead silence, until someone called out, 'What have they decided about the cuts?'

'I don't know,' the Inspector said. 'And now may I suggest that the best thing for you all to do would be to disperse and go home.'

Most of them, including the group with the banners, after

a little hesitation reluctantly began to leave. Kevin said to Jack Bailey, 'We'll do better still outside the Borough Council's HQ tomorrow.'

'Yes,' Jack said. 'See you both there.'

When he had walked off, Kevin asked Mavis, 'Have you ever had lunch at the God's Providence Restaurant?'

'No, I've never tried it,' she said, 'though I've been intrigued by its peculiar name.'

'I had lunch there once,' he said, 'and I thought the food was pretty good. But as for the name, I know no more about its origin than you seem to.'

'I know of a legend,' she said, 'that some hundreds of years ago the people living in a building on this site survived a deadly plague which exterminated the rest of the then small population of the village.'

'It's interesting that this rather plush and populous suburb is still called The Village,' he said, 'and that it is suffering from a plague once again now.'

'I assume you don't mean influenza?'

'No', he said, 'nor bubonic. I mean the plague of Government cuts, of course, which could become deadly for the education and health-care of the majority of the population here as well as in the rest of the country.'

'But we shall do all we can to incite the majority here to resist.'

'Yes,' he said, 'though we shall require refreshment from time to time to keep up our strength. We needn't feel uneasy about that.'

She laughed.

He took her arm and held it till they reached the doors of the God's Providence Restaurant.

They had a table to themselves, and she was aware that he was glad to see she enjoyed their meal as much as he did. She was aware too that, though he must have realised she was at least twenty years older than himself, she had become attractive to him in a way that was more than just comradely. And she found his young handsomeness deeply appealing, without being put off at all by the thought that she was hardly likely to be the first woman who had fallen in love with him.

They finished their meal and he agreed that they should share equally in paying for it.

Then after they'd come out of the Restaurant they stood together in silence for more than a moment. He waited for her to speak first, which she eventually did: 'Well, we have had a wonderful meal today, and we can look forward to meeting again at the demonstration outside the Borough Council Headquarters tomorrow.'

'And I shall return now to my office,' he said, not quite able to hide in his goodbye smile a disappointment he couldn't help feeling. 'I have plenty of work to do.'

'I'm sure you have.'

He had told her during the first of their leafletting expeditions together that he was a solicitor working on his own and specialising in the defence of mainly 'ethnic' victims of unjust arrest by the police. On another such expedition he had also told her that he worked in a small office, with a bedsitter attached, on the third floor of a very large building rather nearer to central London than The Village was. She took the risk of being thought over-curious and asked whether he had a home anywhere. He answered readily enough that he was welcome to go and stay at any time with his parents who had recently retired to a pleasant house in Hampshire.

Now as he smiled his goodbye smile she had difficulty in resisting an impulse to relent and to ask him if he would come back to her small suburban house with her. But she was afraid, while aware she had no clear reason to be so, that too precipitate a start might put at risk the more lasting relationship she longed for with him, and might have an equally precipitate ending.

Yet when she reached her house and stepped inside it a loneliness arose within her such as she had not felt since her husband's death in a road accident ten years before – though then her young son remained for her to look after, so she could not feel wholly alone. But since that time her son had married and gone to a promising job abroad.

Becoming conscious that she was standing rigidly in the middle of the sitting-room of her house, she moved towards one of her comfortable – and expensive – armchairs. (She had never been short of money, and had felt no guilt about it as it had enabled her to help all the better the political cause that meant more than anything else in life to her). She must relax, and because she couldn't do that if she allowed herself to think of Kevin she would try to put him out of her mind by making herself remember her former lover Robert Sheldon, now dead.

Robert had always looked younger than his age, and at seventy-five when he came to live with her after his wife Emma died he had the appearance and the energy of a man of sixty. They agreed that Emma, a friend of hers even as long ago as before she met her own husband, would have been glad that she and Robert had decided to live together.

Her early friendship with Emma, who was considerably older than herself, had arisen from their meeting while engaged in the kind of political activities that made age and class and colour differences between the participants an advantange rather than a hindrance, since they were all members of U C A R, the United Campaign Against Racism, and the more widely inclusive its membership was the stronger it would be. The death of Robert was a third bereavement for her, which she knew could be bearable only if she continued supporting the political struggle that Emma and he had both given so much of the best of their strength to.

But if she was to pass the time tolerably between early afternoon and tomorrow morning's demonstration she would have to do something else besides thinking about the attitude she should adopt towards her bereavement.

The idea came to her that it might be useful if she decided to go and look at the building outside which she and the rest of the group would be demonstrating next morning. She hadn't yet taken off the coat she'd been wearing when she reached her house after saying goodbye to Kevin. Now she tied a light scarf round her head and was soon on her way to a nearby bus-stop, where a bus arrived almost at once which transported her to a street quite close to the Borough Council's HQ.

She found that her memory of the shape of the building was incorrect. The main entrance with the clock high above it jutted out on to the pavement like the bow of a big ship (though without the rising outward curve that the ship's bow would have had), and showed little resemblance to the flattened corner of a large square block that her mind had pictured. The actual shape, broadening from the front to the rear at an angle of perhaps little more than thirty degrees on either side like an arrow-head or the backward-spreading wave that a fast moving ship would create, might present certain strategic difficulties unforeseen by the group before tomorrow's demonstration. It could mean that the crowd would be split into two separated halves along the sides of the building and that this would make them more vulnerable to attacks by the police. Or on the other hand it could possibly enable the crowd to divide the police and drive them back. She felt very ignorant, and also she felt that there was an urgent necessity for the group to discuss tactics before tomorrow.

She had to wait many minutes for a bus that would take her back to her suburb, and when she at last got into her house again she was hesitant for a while about telephoning Kevin. She made herself a cup of tea first. Then she wondered whether to phone Jack Bailey rather than Kevin. But finally she chose Kevin, and she avoided raising any mistaken expectations in him by immediately proposing they should call a meeting, at her house that evening, of as many members of their group as they could contact.

Between them they managed to get on to most of the group, Kevin going to the houses or flats of those who had no phones. It took some time before all who had been contacted arrived, and when they did the discussion lasted until late in the evening. A decision was reached that the tactics they adopted would have to depend on the situation as they found it outside the HQ tomorrow. 'We shall have to play it by ear,' Jack Bailey said.

They seemed disposed to remain longer in her house, just chatting; but at last Kevin decisively said, 'I think we should leave Mavis on her own now to get a good night's rest.'

She made no pretence of wanting to detain them.

• • •

IT BECAME EVIDENT to her as soon as she left the house next morning that something abnormal must be happening in the Borough. The suburban street outside the house, which ordinarily even during rush hours was not excessively used by commuters driving cars, was now completely blocked with stationary vehicles of various kinds. She was glad she was accustomed to get about on foot – in fact she'd never bought a car, not wishing to add to the pollution caused by car exhausts – and she was able to make her way along side pavements towards the Borough Council's HQ. She had increasing difficulty, however, in continuing to move. As the entrance, jutting out like a ship's bow, came into view, she found herself at the back of a thickening crowd which soon brought her to a stop. She was sure that none of her group, not even Jack Bailey, could possibly have got into the Borough Council's public gallery through this crowd. And, as a further obstacle, right at the front of the crowd and just above their heads a long row of police helmets was visible. Every now and then a ripple passed along the row as the crowd's pressure against the police surged and was then held again. More police were continually arriving. There was no sign yet of the Councillors. They were a more reactionary lot than those she and Kevin and their group had demonstrated against in front of the local Town Hall on the previous day. They willingly and keenly carried out the cuts that the Government required, even exceeding the Government's requirements. They had been called the Government's 'Flagship' by certain journalists, and the name had stuck. Quite a number of the crowd here today must have voted for the most objectionable members of this Council at the last elections, but they weren't so stupid as to be unaware of having been betrayed. And they were soon to show how much they resented this.

As the first of five or six of the Councillors were seen walking up the steps to the entrance of the building, trying to give the appearance of not hurrying at all, the foremost members of the crowd were impelled by the mass pressure from those behind them to burst through the quadrupled ranks of foot police now quite unable to protect the rest of the Councillors, who had given up all pretence of not being in a hurry to enter the building. Yet Mavis could see no sign that the crowd, though roaring out protests against their policies, were beginning to attack them physically. Then suddenly the mounted police arrived and set about the crowd with long batons drawn from leather holsters attached to the saddles of their horses. People were being injured, and one of the horses fell, throwing its rider to the ground among the crowd which had begun to stampede. At this moment Mavis and Kevin saw each other. They managed to meet, and he said to her, 'I don't think there would be much point in your staying on here any longer. Let me see you home to your house.'

She willingly agreed. He took her arm and they successfully extricated themselves from the crowd, but when they reached the house he would not come in with her.

'I must go back at once. For professional reasons I need to witness as much as I can of what the police are doing.'

'I shall be worrying about you,' she said. 'I want you to come home here to me as soon as it's all over and you are safely out of it.'

'I will do that,' he said.

• • •

SEVERAL HOURS LATER he still had not returned. She decided it would be better to start preparing an evening meal for them both than just to sit waiting and listening to the occasional crudely biased news bulletin on the radio, and becoming more and more anxious.

She cooked the meal and left it in a low-burning oven to keep it warm. She laid the table for two in her small dining-room. She went to the front door and unlatched it so that he would be able to walk straight in when he arrived, if he did arrive. The possibility that he might not was beginning to seem a likelihood to her when he actually and suddenly did.

'Oh thank goodness you are here,' she said. They moved towards each other, and without any hesitation at all on the part of either of them they embraced and lovingly kissed.

He was the first to sit down. 'I have been very lucky to escape arrest,' he said. 'The police weren't content with picking out and seizing some of the more vociferous among the demonstrators; they pursued others all the way back to their homes. I somehow evaded them – they know me as a solicitor who has successfully defended clients of mine against their trumped-up accusations, and they would have loved to catch me among the demonstrating crowd today. But I got back safely to my office and without turning the lights on I waited for well over an hour before I came out, and when I did I took a devious route to your house. I would have noticed if anyone had been following me.'

He had chosen her sofa to sit down on so that she would be able to sit beside him, which she did.

'And now you are here with me at last,' she said, 'and I have a warm meal waiting in the oven for you.'

She was the first to stand up. Then as he too stood up he said, 'If we were in the best society you would be taking my arm.'

'But as we aren't, you can take mine,' she said.

They sat facing each after she had brought plates piled with food from the oven and set them on the table. He ate hungrily.

'You cook very nicely,' he said. 'This nut-roast, if that's the right name for it, is really delicious.'

'I'm glad you say that. I'm afraid I've rather got out of practice lately. I feel no incentive to take any trouble when I cook only for myself.'

'I find cooking for myself a positive bore,' he said, 'and I don't think I could do much better at it even if I were also cooking for someone else.'

'I shall try to teach you.' She laughed. 'Meanwhile would you like some wine? I ought to have asked you at the beginning of the meal but I haven't drunk any since Robert's time and I'd forgotten that there are a few bottles here in the house still. It's Bulgarian — inexpensive, and I liked the taste of it.'

'I would love to have some.'

She went out to the kitchen and returned with a bottle, two glasses and a corkscrew.

He offered to open the bottle for her.

'Oh no,' she said, 'this is a very special corkscrew and I want to demonstrate how easy it is to use.'

She placed an amber-coloured plastic clamp over the neck of the bottle and then through an aperture at the top of the clamp she inserted a corksrew with an amber-coloured handle into the cork and turned the handle until the clamp began to tighten round the bottle's neck and the cork rose quickly out.

'That plastic must be very strong,' he said.

'Very,' she agreed. Then she poured a little of the wine into her glass, sniffed it, showed satisfaction and, after filling Kevin's glass two-thirds full, topped her own up to the same level.

'You would have made a good wine waitress,' he said.

They touched glasses, looking into each other's eyes.

'It *is* good,' he said after drinking a small quantity. He then began to talk about something which was evidently much on his mind.

'The situation has become extremely dangerous,' he said. 'Tomorrow the crowds in the streets leading to Parliament will be immense, I'm sure, and there's no knowing what lengths the police may go to in trying to cope with them. People are quite likely to be seriously injured and some could be killed.'

'It might happen to you or me or both of us, in fact.'

'Yes.'

'Very well, we can at least go to bed with each other tonight,' she said. 'But you must help me with the washing-up first. We wouldn't want to find that waiting for us in the morning.'

She handed him a large tray and, while she filled a bowl in the kitchen sink with almost boiling-hot water into which she spurted a sprinkling of blue washing-up liquid, he managed fairly quickly to put the plates, knives, forks, glasses and the very special corkscrew on to the tray and to carry it into the kitchen to her.

'Now you can go and wipe the table,' she said, handing him a hot wet cloth. (The table had a hard plastic surface – she disapproved of tablecloths, because they needed washing and ironing.)

She smiled at him when he brought the cloth back to her. She was aware that he liked being ordered about by her.

When they'd finished with the washing-up and drying they sat down side by side on the sofa for a short while.

'I think you'd better use the shower-room first and get into bed first,' she said.

'That will be fine by me.'

'I'll provide you with a nice warm towel and you can hang

your clothes on the chair beside the bed or in the wardrobe, whichever you choose.'

'Lovely,' he said.

'I'll go upstairs now and get things ready for you, and when I've done that I'll come down again and you can go up. Call out to me when you are ready.'

'My angel,' he said.

It wasn't long before he called out, and it wasn't long then before she was upstairs again and had finished preparing herself in the shower-room.

She walked naked into the bedroom, knowing how beautiful her body still looked in spite of her age.

As she got into the bed with him she said, 'Let us just lie side by side for a while together, holding hands.'

He obeyed, but soon he amusedly and quietly asked, 'Have you ever suggested this to anyone else before?'

'No,' she answered, with a laugh, 'but a true lover shouldn't ask such questions – though since you've dared to I'm going to ask you one: How many women have you been to bed with before?'

'I'm honestly not quite sure.'

'You seem to be implying that there were a lot of them.'

'I admit there were, but none of them ever came to mean very much to me.'

'Whereas I do?'

'Yes, you do, you do.'

'Well, I'll believe you, though thousands wouldn't.'

After saying this she felt it was time to put an end to verbal foreplay, and she sensed that he felt the same as she did.

They lay silent side by side holding hands. A delight grew within her and also, she did not doubt, within him. But, gradually, delectable expectation became hot passion and they could restrain themselves no longer.

Turning face to face they closed with each other and he entered her, but she slid an arm round his slim buttocks and held him so tightly against her body that he was unable to make any further movement. Little by little she lessened the pressure of her arm until she became certain he was beginning to understand the desire she had now that he should remain in her for as long as possible with the minimum of movement. He understood; and soon she was aware that this prolonged postponement of what she knew could not be endlessly postponed was making him feel an intensifying joy equal to her own.

At last they could not hold out against the inevitable climax any longer, and they reached it together.

Afterwards they lay side by side again, very close to each other, and happy. Soon they fell deeply asleep, how soon she did not know, but just before she lost consciousness the thought came to her that happiness of every kind was what the political fight should above all be for, and that any sacrifice would be worth while which could help to make it possible among the exploited human millions all over the world who had never known it.

· · ·

THEY WOKE LATE. 'There's no time for breakfast if we are to get anywhere near Parliament this morning,' he said. 'Let us just dress as quickly as we can and stuff a little bread and cheese and an orange into our pockets, or in your case it will be your handbag I suppose, and then leave the house, shutting the front door firmly behind us.'

His plan did not work out quite as he had hoped. They took with them the provisions he had suggested, but as soon as they left the house they found themselves irresistibly drawn into a purpose-fully and one-directionally moving crowd, mainly of men, though Mavis was able to catch sight of quite a few women, two of them being girls who looked as though they might not be out of their teens yet and who each pushed a pram with a baby in it. Soon the movement of the crowd far ahead appeared to Mavis to be gradually slowing down, whilst that part of it which included her and Kevin continued trying to advance without slackening its pace at all and was becoming increasingly compressed. She began to wonder how much more of this her body would be capable of bearing; but eventually the whole crowd, those coming up from the far rear as well as those in front began to slow down, and the pressure on her was eased. Word must have been passed back to the rearmost of these demonstrators that their foremost members were joining in with a much larger contingent of demonstrators who were moving only a little less slowly along a road which was broader than theirs. It was like a lively tributary meeting a sluggishly advancing river, Mavis thought, though there was nothing sluggish about the feelings against the Government that the demonstrators were loudly expressing. Soon the river met an even broader one and all movement stopped, except that of clenched fists raised high above the shouting faces. It was as though people who for years had more or less passively put up with the injustices, insults, ever increasing impoverishment while the rich grew continually richer, and all the rest of the evils that the Government with arrogant impunity had inflicted on them, were now suddenly and simultaneously and ubiquitously inspired with a determination to put an end to it and to the power of those responsible for it. Mavis turned to share these thoughts of hers with Kevin, but she discovered that he was no longer at her side. The crowd had somehow enveloped him, and she could catch no glimpse of him among them.

There must be thousands on thousands of them here, perhaps a million. What could the riot police with their shields or the mounted police with their long batons do to quell them? What even could rifle-firing soldiers do, beyond killing a considerable number of them and thereby further enraging the vast majority who continued to survive? Someone with a portable phone suddenly announced through a megaphone, 'I have just had a message that the whole of Liverpool have come out like us.' A tremendous cheer went up from the crowd. After this, minute by minute similar messages came in from all the main towns in England, in Wales, in Scotland, in Ireland; then all at once a new voice speaking also through a megaphone told the crowd, 'The whole of South America has now come out in support of us.' And the same voice soon added, 'I've just heard that an imperialist fleet of giant North American troop carriers has been prevented by the ground staff from taking to the air.' Then a young man, who also held a megaphone, was lifted up somehow from the middle of the crowd and exclaimed passionately, 'Comrades, the World Revolution has begun.'

It was at this moment that Mavis found Jack Bailey standing at her side. 'I thought you were lost,' he said. 'So did I,' she said, 'and I'm glad to see you.'

'Well, now I can tell you something that you may not have realised and ought to know. Nearly all the speakers are police provocateurs, with the probable exception of the young man who shouted that the World Revolution had begun. I would guess he is a member of one of those small groups that are genuinely social-ist, but overoptimistic. As for my own belief, I have never doubted that the revolution will eventually come, though not in my life-time; yet on the other hand I cannot be certain that it might not come sooner.'

As he said this she felt a sudden heavy thud against the back of her shoulder, and a sharp pain. 'I think I may have been shot,' she was just able to say. Then she knew no more.

• • •

AFTER THE DEMONSTRATION outside the local Town Hall, during which the demonstrators had shouted, 'SAVE OUR COTTAGE HOSPITAL' and 'SAVE OUR VILLAGE SCHOOL', Kevin had been puzzled by the absence of Mavis who he knew to have been particularly keen to be there. He decided to go along to her house to find out why she had not come.

A bottle of milk had not been taken in from outside her front door. He knocked on her door several times and he rang her bell several times but got no answer. He felt sufficiently uneasy to contact the police, a thing he did not like to do. They came and broke open her door, and followed by Kevin they went up to her bedroom where they found her lying dead in her bed.

It was not her influenza that had been a dream.

EMILY AND OSWIN

A 65-YEAR-OLD well-to-do widow, Mrs Emily Harlowe, was glancing through her newspaper *The Daily Messenger* one morning when she came upon a brief paragraph stating that the poet Oswin Walden was now in a 'home' for old people. (Normally *The Daily Messenger* ignored Walden's existence – the editor and the notably rapacious proprietor of this 'quality' newspaper both detested him because of his politics – however his present misfortune was presumably not displeasing to them and the editor had considered it worthy of mention.) Emily liked poetry, and the few poems by him she had read in magazines and newspapers that published poetry had been more interesting to her than most of those they published by other poets. The paragraph about him in *The Daily Messenger* was strangely disturbing to her; and, as the days went by, a wish grew in her to do something to help him.

For quite a while now she had felt increasingly dissatisfied with the life she was living, in spite of the various pleasures it gave her – such as playing bridge several afternoons each week with local women friends, helping the amiable local vicar by doing flower arrangements (she could do these quite expertly) for special occasions at his church, and getting regular visits from her married daughters who lived in the north of England and brought with them their likeable children, her grandchildren. But she at last came to recognise with hardly any shame that what she needed above everything else was to have some excitement in her life before it was too late. She decided that she would try to rescue Oswin Walden from a 'home' which she didn't doubt he must abominate.

The paragraph in *The Daily Messenger* had been unhelpfully imprecise as a guide to the whereabouts of the 'home', stating merely that it was in Sussex. She wrote to the editor saying she would be grateful if he could give her its address, and after a long delay his secretary answered that it was near Eastbourne and that it was called 'Sundown House'.

She told her friends she was going for a holiday in Sussex; and early one midweek morning, before the commuter traffic started from the London suburb where she and they lived, she packed her suitcase and set out in her expensive new Rover car to drive south via the Dartford crossing towards Eastbourne.

Sundown House was not too difficult for her to find. It was on a main road and its name was painted large over its front door. She parked her car in a side road and walked to the door and rang the bell. She had to wait what seemed more than a minute before the door was opened to her by a young woman dressed in clothes that made no pretence of resembling those of a trained nurse. When Emily asked to see Mr Oswin Walden, the young woman gave her a nervously doubtful look. 'I'll ask Mr Imray,' she said.

Mr Imray, tall in a smart gray suit, came quickly down a curving flight of stairs towards Emily. He had evidently overheard from above what she'd said to the young woman.

With a look of undisguised suspicion he asked her, 'Are you an investigative journalist?'

'No', Emily said, surprised, and then becoming suspicious herself she said, 'Why do you ask? Is there something here that you would rather not have investigated?'

'Of course there isn't,' he said, 'but all of us who run private residential homes mainly for the elderly are on the alert against freelance journalists intending to get sensational reports about us published in the tabloid press.'

'You can set your mind at rest as to my intentions,' she said. 'I am simply someone who admires Oswin Walden's poetry, and

I would like to meet him and to see if I can do anything to help him.'

'Would you mind telling me your name?'

'Mrs Howarth.'

'Very well,' Mr Imray said, 'I'll go and ask him.'

Imray was soon back again, saying, 'He's quite indifferent whether he sees you or not.'

'I would like to see him,' Emily said.

Imray led her along a passageway which had a number of similar-seeming doors on either side of it. He stopped at one of these and without knocking on it he showed her into a room where Oswin Walden was sitting in an armchair, wearing pyjamas and a dressing-gown and holding a closed notebook on his lap.

Imray went out of the room without completely shutting the door, and she was left alone with the poet.

'I hope you don't mind my intruding on you,' she said, 'but I am an admirer of your poetry, and when I read in *The Messenger* that you were in this home I felt I must come down here to see if I could be of any use to you.'

He said nothing.

There was a second armchair near his, and after some hesitation she sat down in it.

'I could get you out of here today at once if you wished.'

'I would have nowhere to go,' he said. 'They have sold my house.'

She gazed at him, and he gazed at her.

He found her attractive to look at, though he judged that she was probably in her middle sixties or older. She did not think him particularly good-looking, but she felt sure that he couldn't be less than thirty years younger than herself.

'Are you given enough to eat here?' she asked him.

'The food is uninteresting, to say the least, and is atrociously cooked, but we are not starved.'

'Wouldn't you like a holiday?'

'A holiday from my present state of mind – yes, I certainly would,' he said with a hint of irony.

'A change of place might help to change your state of mind,' she said.

'A change of place could even worsen my state of mind,' he said. 'I might feel wholly lost and disorientated.'

'I could take you to a place of your own choice which you've known well and liked in the past and where you would not feel disorientated at all,' she said.

'I can't think of any such place,' he said, 'though I might like Rouen. Before the War my elder brother stayed several months there, and he was enthusiastic about it.'

'All right, we will travel there tomorrow.'

Oswin looked at her with disbelief.

'Where are your outdoor clothes?' she asked.

'Imray keeps them locked away.'

'I'll get them from him.' She stood up and walked quickly out of the room.

Imray asked what right she thought she had to remove one of his residents from here. For all he knew she might be a member of one those pseudo-religious cults that would submit him to a repulsive 'cure' which would convert his neurosis into real insanity. 'I may be exaggerating,' Imray said, 'but you can appreciate why I am not keen to let him be taken from Sundown House by someone I know nothing about.'

'I can appreciate that you are not keen to lose the money you are paid for keeping him here,' she said, 'but I have several influential friends, and I think that if I were to give them a not entirely unfavourable report on the running of Sundown House you might feel sufficiently compensated.'

Without a word he went from the room to fetch Oswin's outdoor clothes. He returned and handed them to her; and she handed them to Oswin, who seemed unwilling to put them on.

Guessing that he did not want to change in her presence she left him alone with Imray.

After a considerable while he emerged fully dressed into the hall, carrying the suitcase that contained the rest of his belongings. Imray in silence ushered Emily and Oswin out of the front door, which he closed behind them.

She led him to her impressive-looking car in the side-street, and opening the large boot at the rear of it she told him to put his suitcase into this next to her own that was already there. Then she got him to sit down in the front seat beside her.

'Where are we going?' he asked as she drove out on to the main road.

'To Southampton,' she said.

During the journey to Southampton she asked him various questions about himself, which she found he was very ready to answer.

One of the first of these was, 'How did it happen that you were sent from your own house to Sundown House?'

Oswin, before answering this, mentioned that his 'house' was really only an ordinary rural cottage, not a house. Then he said, 'It happened when I got myself into such a neurotic state that a retired pharmacist, Mr Robinson, who lived in a nearby cottage and occasionally looked in on me for a brief neighbourly chat, went to see the local GP, Dr Parsons, about me. I willingly agreed to be visited by Dr Parsons, but after he'd asked me various questions he was uncertain what should be done with me. I didn't seem to be the sort of case he should send to a mental hospital, but on the other hand he felt I couldn't just be left where I was. Finally I accepted a suggestion of his that I should go into Sundown House at least temporarily. I didn't foresee that during the time I was there my cottage would be sold to help pay for my keep.'

'What made you get yourself into such a neurotic state?'

'I was trying every day and all day to write a better kind of poetry than I'd written before, and I wasn't succeeding. I drove myself harder and harder, and at last several nights came when I couldn't sleep at all. It was then that Robinson asked Parsons to come and visit me.'

'Were you able to sleep at Sundown House?'

'Oh yes; they gave me dope. I've still got quite a lot with me now. But I always managed to avoid taking any in the daytime, however bad I felt.'

'There was a closed notebook on your lap when I first saw you. Do you mind my asking whether you still hope to write a poem of the new kind you wanted to?'

'I think I do. But I haven't yet got any farther than occasionally discussing in my notebook what was wrong with my previous attempts.'

She asked him what he thought was wrong with his previous attempts.

He explained that they were still too explicitly political. What he aimed to do was to write poems which though they would most of them continue to be political would never be other than implicitly so.

'I suppose I've realised that the poems of yours I've read and admired were explicitly political, but this didn't bother me in the least,' she said. 'For me the impressive thing about them was how well they were written and how comprehensible they were.'

He noticed that all the while she was speaking she kept a careful eye on the road. She was a good driver, better than he had been when he had owned a car (an antiquated third-hand one).

She went on to ask him at what age he became a poet.

He found himself speaking freely to her about his boyhood and his social origins. He was born in 1924 in an Essex town within twelve miles of London. His father, he told her, was a railway signalman and his mother a teacher whose parents had been working-class. His elder brother, Henry, their only other child, was four years older than him. They went to the same elementary school, and both did well there, Henry going on to a good secondary school where he was quite happy, and Oswin to a posh grammar school where he was made to feel socially inferior, though he did well academically. While he was there he fell in love with a middle-class girl at a girls' high school in the same town, and the first poem he ever wrote was a love poem inspired by her, but he never dared to show it to her or to tell her he was in love with her. Henry was killed early on in the 1939 war. Oswin himself was called up in 1942 and joined the fire service. In 1945 after the war he was able to go to a redbrick university where he got a good degree in English. He left in 1948 at the age of 24 and he earned a bare living for some years as a journalist writing under an assumed name for a local newspaper whose proprietor could be described as a liberal Tory. He had two books of his poems published by a reputable publisher which were reviewed dismissively or hostilely in several 'quality' papers and magazines, but he got good reviews from two reviewers who thought him promising.

Abruptly he stopped talking, afraid that he might have been boring her and that she wasn't really listening. But she had been listening with sympathetic interest and she asked him to go on.

He told her that he had never got married, and why. He had had affairs with three women, but found he'd not enough in common with any of the three to want to settle down with her. Then he had fallen quite seriously in love with a fourth and would have liked to marry her, but he discovered he was sharing her with another man of his own age who had a better income than his and who did eventually marry her. It was soon after this that his mother died (his father had died a year earlier) and she left him a little money, which helped him to buy the quiet cottage in Sussex where he hoped to concentrate on solving his poetic problem.

All at once Oswin became conscious that he knew nothing about the life of the woman he had been speaking to so unreservedly about his own life, and who had chosen to drive him to Southampton in her car now.

He decided to ask her to tell him about herself.

She readily did. 'I am the widow of a workaholic,' she said. 'Don't misunderstand me. Charles was a good husband to me, as the saying goes, and I had two lovely children by him, but he was the chairman of an important company and more of his time and energy was given to his work than he was physically able to bear. One morning not more than an hour after he had said goodbye to me and left the house, his secretary rang up to tell me he had died suddenly of heart failure while at work.'

'How dreadfully upsetting for you,' Oswin said.

'Yes, the immediate shock was dreadful, but my daughters who by then had grown up and got married were very supportive – so were my friends – and I felt almost ashamed that I recovered from it as soon as I did.'

'Though after recovering from it you must have had a feeling of loss which you couldn't recover from so soon,' Oswin said, sympathetically.

'I have to admit that I didn't grieve as greatly for him as I expected to. I suppose the truth is I never deeply loved him,' she said. 'I thought just as my parents did that he would be a suitable husband for me because he was very well-off, and so were they. "Money marries money" was one of my father's favourite sayings. And I didn't find Charles actually unattractive. He was about the same age as I was, quite good-looking, and very considerate.'

Oswin was astonished at her having, casually almost, revealed all this about her married life to him. He would have liked to ask whether she had ever at any time fallen in love with anyone, but he dared not.

A silence, except for occasional remarks about the scenery or the behaviour of other motorists on the road, fell between them during the rest of their drive to Southampton.

Emily stopped her car in a parking-space that fronted an expensive-looking hotel. After getting out from her driving seat she opened the car door for him on his side of the car and then went to unlock the car boot where their suitcases were. She told him to follow her into the hotel, but Oswin, wishing to be to helpful, lifted the two suitcases from the boot and was about to carry them into the hotel.

'No,' she said peremptorily. 'A servant from the hotel can do that.'

He put the cases down and followed her into the entrance hall of the hotel, where she approached a young woman who sat at a desk to which was affixed the word 'Reception', printed in gold on a wavy-edged piece of polished brown wood. Emily announced that she wanted two separate rooms. She wrote her name and address in the visitors' book, and Oswin wrote his name, but he hesitated a moment before deciding to give Sundown House as his address. Then, after the Receptionist had presented her with the key for room number 7, and Oswin with the key for number 8, Emily asked that the two suitcases which were standing close to the boot of her black Rover car in the forecourt should be brought into the hotel at once.

A uniformed young man carried the cases up a short flight of stairs, and deposited them in rooms 7 and 8, Emily and Oswin having unlocked the doors for him. Emily gave the man a tip, and this slightly embarrassed Oswin who couldn't help feeling that in paying for his stay at this hotel she would be giving him a kind of tip.

Emily went into her room and Oswin went into his, where quite soon, however, she joined him.

'Well, what do you think of it?' she asked.

Oswin didn't immediately know what to say he thought of it, but he was aware that it was an 'en suite' room and that beyond the rather broad chintzy single bed there was a smaller room containing a wash-basin, a shower, and a 'toilet'.

'I think I'll take advantage of the facilities here,' he said.

'That's a good idea,' she said. 'I'll return to my room and do likewise. Then we will go downstairs together to find out when dinner is served.'

They walked down the wide stairs side by side, she holding his arm and wearing an evening dress, low-cut and with what looked like a triple diamond necklace (presumably the diamonds weren't real) partially covering her neck; whereas he wore the everyday, far from smart or even very clean, clothes he had been wearing on the day he had been taken from his cottage to Sundown House.

Emily asked the Receptionist what time dinner would be served. 'Within twenty minutes,' the Receptionist said, 'and meanwhile perhaps you might like to go and sit in the lounge through the arch over there.' She pointed to the arch. Emily detected a hint of disrespect in the Receptionist's manner, but deciding to appear not to have noticed it she was soon leading Oswin through the arch into a lounge which was already quite crowded with guests of both sexes, who all of them seemed to Oswin to be as well-dressed for dinner as Emily was.

'I can't help feeling a bit out of place here in these clothes of mine,' he murmured to her only semi-humorously.

She turned on him with more than semi-serious scorn: 'So much for your explicit or implicit political principles,' she said. 'You ought not to care a damn about what these no doubt mostly Conservative types here may think of the way you are dressed.'

'You are right,' he said contritely.

'Very well,' she said, 'I'll let you do penance by buying the drinks for us both. I know you've got just about enough money of your own to buy them with. And if your conduct improves in future, I may even consider recoupling you.'

'What will you have?' he asked her.

'A large gin-and-tonic,' she said.

He went to the bar and bought this for her and a schooner of dry sherry for himself. He felt better after drinking the sherry, and when she had finished her gin-and-tonic he wanted to go and buy a repeat for her and for himself, but she would not let him.

However, between them they drank a whole bottle of excellent Burgundy with their tolerably good dinner. At the end of it she said, 'I don't feel much like retiring to the lounge now, do you? I think bed might be best after our long drive today.'

'Yes, I agree it might be,' he said.

They went up the broad stairway together, ignoring the Receptionist who was still at her desk.

Outside their rooms they stopped and turned to face each other.

'Well, good-night, Oswin,' she said.

'Good-night,' he said.

She went into her room and he went into his.

He gave himself a shower; after which he put on his pyjamas and got into his chintzily coverleted hotel bed. It was comfortable, but he had no intention of trying to go to sleep in it. He waited for a time that he calculated would be long enough to allow Emily to finish her preparations and to get into the bed in her room. Then, with his dressing gown on over his pyjamas, he cautiously opened his door to make sure that none of the other guests was in the passageway. He saw no one. He hurried to her door, quickly and quietly opened it and was inside her room.

She was sitting up in her bed wearing a silk nightgown. She looked relieved and glad to see him.

'I hoped this would happen,' she said.

He took off his dressing gown, placed it on a bedside chair and got into bed with her. He had a strange feeling that now he would be able to avenge himself for some of the humiliations she had inflicted on him. He embraced her and she held him tight against her, almost as though to prevent him from making any further movement. As though she feared it. And she did suddenly fear being inadequate after her many years of sexless widowhood. But he was gentle with her, and her fears gave way to a prolonged intense delight such as she had never experienced with Charles. It was repeated several times that night, and she knew when they woke in the morning that she was helplessly in love with him.

She drove him in her car to an AA-approved garage where it could remain until they returned from Rouen. They then walked arm-in-arm together along the streets of Southampton, window-shopping and also visiting the ancient Guildhall and the Maritime Museum. They had lunch together in a famous pub, where she was unwise enough after drinking two glasses of red wine with her meal to make the would-be humorous remark that some of the other eaters present might refer to him among themselves as her 'toy-boy'.

He was angry with her, and said, 'Perhaps that's how you too think of me.'

'Oh no, Oswin,' she said, distressed. 'I love you.'

He said nothing. He felt embarrassed.

But they had got over the tiff between them by the time they came to the ticket office where she booked two first-class berths on the boat which was to take them on the six-hour night crossing from Southampton to Le Havre.

They arrived early in the morning and were drowsy during their comfortable train journey to Rouen.

'French trains were very different in my brother Henry's day,' Oswin told her. 'He used to say that when they were going at speed they rocked from side to side and he was terrified that they might come off the rails at any moment. But it seems that nowadays they are more comfortable and less alarming than the English trains are.'

'You could be right about that,' she said, 'though you're judging only by your experience of the one French train we are on at present.'

'I do think that English railways are less efficient than they were in my father's day,' he said, 'and I think that the Government's deliberate policy of favouring the roads at the expense of the railways is to blame for it.'

'If the English railways have become less efficient it's the fault of the people who manage them and not of the Government's pro-road policy,' she told him.

'There are times when I get the impression that you are politically a little bit reactionary,' he said mildly.

'No,' she said. 'I'm just an unpolitical person who likes owning and driving an up-to-date car.'

They took a taxi from the station at Rouen to a large and newly-built hotel recommended by the proprietor of the garage in Southampton where Emily had left her car. (Oswin wondered whether the Hôtel de la Poste, which his brother Henry had spoken of as being favoured by English tourists, still existed.) A guide-book obtained by Emily at the new hotel told her and Oswin how severely the city had been damaged during the war, and proudly stressed the recent reconstruction of a number of its famous medieval buildings. Mostly these were what they spent their next few days in going to see. First its two cathedrals, the 14th-century Abbey Church of St-Ouen and the 13th to 16th-century gothic Notre-Dame with the high green metal spire inside which a winding stair rose towards the summit. From this stair Henry had released over the city a piece of lavatory paper inscribed with a blasphemous statement capable of getting him into serious trouble if it had floated down into hostile hands. (Henry ashamedly admitted to Oswin that he was then, like many another British contemporary of his, little more than an overgrown schoolboy compared with the adult-minded continental young men of approximately his own age he would soon meet.) Emily was keen also to see La Tour Jeanne d'Arc, the tower where Joan of Arc was, incorrectly perhaps, said to have been imprisoned for a while before being burnt at the stake, but what interested Oswin more than La Tour was Le Gros-Horloge – because this big ornate clock was above a narrow street in which there had been a restaurant where Henry had eaten artichokes that he claimed had poisoned him for three days. However, there was something Oswin was keener to see than anything else unmentioned in the guide-book – a 'pension' with the address 'Le Vert Logis, Impasse des Arquebusiers, Boulevard St-Hilaire'. Henry had once told Oswin that during his stay here he was happier than he had ever been before.

Yet Oswin shrank from telling Emily that he wanted to see it. He was afraid of the deep disappointment he would feel if he found that it was no longer there. The map in the guide-book clearly showed the Boulevard St-Hilaire, but not the Impasse des Arquebusiers.

He did not tell her and they did not try to find it. His mind however was dominated by thoughts and feelings about it wherever they went. She was well aware that he wasn't fully attentive to what they were actually seeing; but also she sensed an exaltation in him, and she forgave him. After all he was a poet, and he might at last be beginning to dream up a poem of the kind he had for so long been unsuccessfully trying to write.

The truth was that Oswin in his imagination, and with the aid of what his brother Henry had told him, had become his brother Henry.

On his first morning at the pension he was woken by a beautiful young girl saying in a gentle voice, 'Bonjour Monsieur', before drawing back his bedroom curtains. (He was soon to discover that she was a peasant girl and a slavey at the beck and call of an astonishing woman rarely seen above stairs who cooked the excellent meals which the girl brought to the pension table.) He seemed from the start to be on a new plane of existence, liberating and superior to almost anything he had ever experienced in England. Even the aroma arising from the bowl of French coffee served at petit déjeuner, and especially the taste of the coffee itself and of the croissant he ate with it, had this same liberating effect on him, so different were they from the cruder though appetising enough smell and flavour of a more substantial English breakfast.

Meeting the other guests at the pension – with the exception of the only Englishman (who was a typical 'public-school' product) – was also exciting to him. There were the three Scandinavians, a Norwegian young woman and two Swedish males, one of them a little older than the other, who played footsie-footsie with her

under the table, and she couldn't refrain from grinning. There was
a young Frenchman, André Poncet, very upright in his bearing,
smartly dressed and precise in pronouncing the words he used,
who mockingly took to calling Henry 'Monsieur le Philosophe'.
But he was friendly too, admitting to Henry that the prospect of
having to do two years' military training in the French army, as
other young Frenchmen of his age also had to, did not please him.
Then a young woman arrived from Finland, with fair hair and a
pretty face, whose surname was Pletchnikov. (Henry never knew
her first name.) Poncet was soon quite often in her room, and the
puritanical English ex-School Prefect, Paget, spied on them. Poncet
one day discovering this was understandably furious.

Poncet worked in the town for a commercial firm, and
occasionally he went home for a couple of days to stay with
his parents. Whenever this happened Pletchnikov was unhappy.
Henry wrote a mocking verse, which to his disgrace he showed to
Paget:

> *Pletchnikov and Poncet*
> *Are flirting all the day*
> *And Pletchnikov is homesick*
> *When Poncet goes away.*

Undoubtedly Paget was envious, but Henry genuinely was not.
What mattered to him more than anything else was his poetry,
and he found that the Vert Logis with its many peculiarities was a
poetically stimulating place to be staying in.

Why did it defy ordinary French grammar by placing the word
'Vert' before instead of after the word 'Logis'? Why, high up at right
angles to the front of the building, was there a garden bright with
shrubs in flower, and immediately below this two heavy wooden
padlocked doors which concealed a cellar containing wine barrels?
Every now and then a lorry with a not very large tank on it
would arrive in the Impasse. The driver would get down from his

driving-seat and, drawing out with one hand from the lorry a long rubber hose, he would unlock with a key in his other hand the big padlock that kept the doors of the cellar closed. Then he would enter the cellar and after unbunging one of the barrels he would suck at that end of the hose until a siphoning process had been established and he could spit out the small quantity of wine that remained in his mouth while he directed its full flow into the bung-hole of the barrel.

But Henry was not sure of having correctly understood what had been happening. Did another lorry perhaps come in the middle of the night to take the full barrels away and replace them with other empty ones? Or might he be even more wrong and might the wine be flowing from the barrels into the tanker?

One of the things he could be certain about was that he was never given wine to drink at the pension. Nor water either, apart from the boiled water with which his morning coffee was presumably made. And at the main meal of the day the guests were always provided with a glass of pink syrupy liquid, likely to be grenadine diluted with cooled water that had been boiled. The proprietors of the pension, Monsieur and Madame Morel, seemed to be as distrustful of the quality of French water as the British then were. At any rate, none of their guests was known to have been afflicted with typhoid after returning home.

Henry, when describing such details to Oswin made clear that for himself they were not trivial. They all in their own way contributed to the special poetic appeal that Rouen had for him. This was true even of the *Vidange*, a lorry that used to be driven round to various houses in Rouen for the purpose of pumping out sewage from domestic cesspits through a long, capacious and flexible metal hose. The hose as it trailed its way out down the stairs of Le Vert Logis leaked slightly, Henry said.

Oswin commented that he couldn't easily understand how the *Vidange* could have much poetic appeal, but Henry answered that

there had been comic scenes in some of the greatest of Marlowe's
and Shakespeare's Tragedies.

•

OFTEN OSWIN had wondered what Henry's feelings had been in
the months preceding the war that was to kill him.

The poetry he wrote at school, and continued to write almost
until the actual outbreak of the war, was unpolitical and showed no
sign of concern about the rise of Nazism in Europe.

•

OSWIN'S EXPERIENCE as a fire fighter during the war had
strengthened his will to write poetry in support of the working-
class he had been born into, but after the war he had failed to write
the kind of poems he wanted to, and if it hadn't been for the help
of a member of the upper-middle class he might have remained in
Sundown House and have become slowly insane.

•

NOW THE TIME had arrived for him and Emily to return from
Rouen to England. What were they going to do when they got
there?

He had avoided asking her while they remained in France, but
she herself raised the subject while they were on the boat back to
Southampton.

She said that to begin with they could stay in the same
Southampton hotel they had stayed in before crossing to France.

'And after that?' he asked.

'I shall find you a house.'

'What about your own house?'

'Quite impossible,' she said with alarm, 'The scandal it would
cause in the village would make our lives there unbearable.'

'Yes, of course it would,' he agreed. 'I was only joking.'

'Where would you like to have a house?'

'Somewhere in or near the Essex town where I was born,' he
said. 'But I wouldn't want it as a gift. I would want to pay you
for it.'

'I could make you an interest-free loan which you could pay off gradually as soon as you could afford to.'

'That is very generous of you,' he said.

•

SOON AFTER THEIR return to England they motored to Oswin's home town. They stayed in a local hotel – at Emily's expense – while visiting various Estate Agents and being taken to look at, and into, various houses that were up for sale. The small house once owned by Oswin's signalman father in which Oswin had been born had now been demolished, but quite near the site of it there was a not-too-large house that Oswin thought suitable. It was the end house of a terrace which was 'on the wrong side of the tracks' (an American phrase meaning 'situated in the lower-class part of the town on the wrong side of the railway'), and he particularly liked to use the phrase because of its conciseness.

•

MUCH OF THE FURNITURE necessary to him – bed, a table, a few chairs – was sold with the house, as were a fridge and various facilities for cooking. Other requirements, including discarded (though by no means too worn) bedclothes and curtains were supplied by Emily, who also gave him a typewriter in good condition that had belonged to her husband.

By means of some private tutoring of teenagers working for exams, and some journalism for the editor of the local newspaper, he was able to keep up his payments to Emily, and she quite often came to see him.

Then he got to know a small group of people whose political views were similar to his own.

Being with them enabled him at last to begin writing the kind of poetry he had for so many months been unsuccessfully trying to write. And after a while he and a young woman in the group, who was younger than himself, fell for each other.

He let Emily know about this, and she wished him well. She even came to meet them both. But she was broken-hearted, and before long she decided to move from her village and to go and end her days in an extremely expensive 'home'.

She found that it had wonderfully spacious grounds and a marvellous view of trees beyond which swans could be seen swimming on a blue sky-reflecting lake. She wrote to describe all this to him, and to tell him that he need no longer continue to pay off the money she had lent him.

•

WHAT SHE WAS never to tell him was that at this 'home' she met a beautiful man, a little older than herself, and that they became platonic lovers.